THE TOBY MY...

BOOK 1

◆ ◆ ◆ ◆ ◆ ◆ ◆ ❖ ◆ ◆ ◆ ◆ ◆ ◆

Finding Toby

Andy Hughes

ISBN 979-8-391469-26-1

This book is a work of fiction and any resemblance to actual events or persons is entirely coincidental

Cover design by Leah Hughes

CHAPTER 1

Inhaling sharply, Toby snatched his bag, yanked down on the handle, and threw his shoulder against the door, bursting out of the helicopter. Leaping to the ground, the teenager landed on all fours, but adrenalin surged through him and he sprang to his feet, dashing across the clearing into the dense jungle. A loud CRACK burst through the whirring of the rotor blades and Toby ducked as he felt a bullet rush past his right ear. His long legs drove him forward, blindly stumbling into the thick undergrowth and through the trees.

Panic kept him moving forward despite his lungs begging him to stop, but he slowed his pace, trying to propel himself forward in a more controlled run, focusing on his breathing. His PE teacher's voice called out to him in his monotone voice: "Steady your pace! Breathe in time to your steps! In … out … in … out!" Toby automatically responded, and his chest pains lessened, but almost as soon as they did, another CRACK pierced the air, and a millisecond later, a bullet whizzed through the leaves past him, stopping somewhere close ahead. Toby was increasing the gap!

"Umph!" Toby was stopped dead as a root grabbed his toe, and he fell hard on his knees. Throwing his hands out, he managed to stop the forward motion of his body from smashing his face into the hard ground, but the force shot pain through his forearms and he cried out. Still in 'fight or flight' mode, he launched himself onto his feet and continued on, oblivious to the blood trickling down his shins.

Huge, broad leaves and thin palms whipped at his bare arms and legs as he headed deeper into the unknown, his only thought: to escape the gunman chasing him.

Just as Toby's lungs began to collapse from the strain, the sound of the helicopter grew inaudible and he could no longer hear the man crashing through the vegetation behind him. He slowed to a jog but fear made him carry on, not daring to stop and look around. Finally, lack of oxygen forced him to stop.

Toby slumped at the base of a huge unrecognisable tree with a buttress base. He could almost hide between the folds of its fortress like trunk. He leaned back against the rough bark, trying to regain his breath, waiting for his heart to go back down to his chest and his jellified legs to solidify. He leaned his head forward and ran his fingers through his short dark hair, wishing he had spent more time doing physical activity instead of sitting in front of his X-box. He looked down at his bloody legs, wiping at them absently, and whispered softly to himself,

"What just happened?" He paused, "Where on earth am I?"

How had he ended up here, wherever 'here' was? His dark eyes looked around him at the unfamiliar trees and plants, trying to make sense of his surroundings. He should be at Aunt Doreen and Uncle Derrick's home in Okotoks, Canada.

Toby had been volunteered by his parents to help his mom's aunt and uncle, much to his annoyance. His great uncle Derrick had broken his leg when he fell off a ladder cleaning the windows of the house they had just purchased. Toby was to help with some painting and other decorating, do a few things in their yard, plus help unpack all their belongings. He had had a fun summer planned with his friend, Adam; hiking and camping in the Brecon Beacons, and had reverted to toddler-like behaviour when his parents had told him the plans they had made without consulting him. Nothing would change their minds, and they had booked the flight despite all his protests.

Toby's thoughts went forward to Heathrow airport. How had he gotten on the wrong plane to here, some hot jungle where a mad man was trying to kill him? He had handed over his passport and ticket at the boarding gate and the woman behind the desk had told him he was at the wrong gate. Looking at her watch, she had quickly grabbed some official looking man who rushed Toby over to some other gate where a stewardess hurried him onto the plane. It was taxiing down the runway only minutes after he had taken his seat.

Toby squinted as he tried to remember past take off. For some reason, sleep had engulfed him pretty much the whole flight and he had still been groggy at touch down, struggling to walk off the plane into what he thought was the Calgary airport, the big city close to where his great aunt and uncle lived.

A mosquito brought Toby back to his surroundings and the oppressive humid air around him. His gaze rested on his bag and suddenly a thought struck him. He reached inside and grabbed his passport, pulling out the ticket that was stuffed inside.

"Managua," he read out loud, "Managua?" Desperately he searched his memory; the name was there faintly somewhere, taunting him, just like his nine year old twin sisters, Samantha and Alexandra did when they were in mischievous moods.

"Nicaragua!" Something shouted in his mind, but it was not his geography teacher, the ominous Mrs Stone, whose face mimicked her name. A picture flashed in his mind of the kid he had met at Heathrow airport: a boy that had looked strikingly like himself: Benito. They had joked about it, because Toby felt he had a pointed nose and oval chin, and thought Benito was a better looking, slightly darker version of himself, with his nose slightly more rounded and his chin more rugged and square. Benito had been going to Nicaragua to visit an Uncle … Tadeo.

Toby looked down at the passport he held in his other hand. He held his breath, as he slowly opened the passport to the picture, but somehow, he knew what he would see. Sure enough, Benito's face stared back at him. Toby gazed at the photo, searching; somehow hoping to find the answers to all his questions. How? Why? Toby looked around him and his eyes were drawn up high to the top of the huge tree against which he leant. What on earth was he supposed to do?

The gruff man who had met him at the airport must have been Benito's uncle. While Toby, still groggy, was trying to explain to the annoyed official at passport control that he had come to Calgary to visit his aunt and uncle, Benito's uncle had come along, whispered harshly in the official's ear and, grabbing Toby's arm, dragged him past security. With his strength finally returning, Toby had tried to release the strong man's tight hold. The man had opened his jacket just enough for him to see a small gun tucked within easy reaching of Tadeo's big hand. Grabbing a large holdall off the luggage belt, the large man had hauled Toby into a waiting taxi and, after shouting at the driver in a foreign language, they travelled a short distance to a huge building with several helicopters lined up on the concrete pad at the front.

Another mosquito brought Toby back to his present position, sitting with his knees pulled close to him, the blood on his dirty legs drying. His breathing had finally returned to normal after his run for survival and an overwhelming thirst consumed him. Reaching in his bag, he grabbed the large water bottle he had had the stewardess fill on the plane. Toby took a deep drink but stopped suddenly as he took in the jungle around him. Where would he find fresh water? He recalled seeing a small river from the helicopter just before they landed. He gazed at the plants and trees, most of which were unfamiliar to him. Would he be able to find his way back to the clearing where they had landed?

As he stopped focusing on his breathing, he noticed the loud, strange birds and other creatures calling out to each other. A bright orange, yellow and blue parrot flew by into the air above him and as his gaze followed the bird up, he saw through the canopy of trees that the dim light was not just due to the thick growth of vegetation. He would have to make plans quickly before the sun set. His stomach growled. There were some crisps and chocolate in his backpack, plus a bag of Murray mints, which would do for one meal. And after that? Toby sighed deeply,

"I should have paid more attention to all those Bear Grylls survival programmes my dad watched," he said out loud.

———◦●◦———

Tadeo cursed as his bullet missed the boy and he disappeared into the jungle. He took chase, but after a short while, he decided to let the jungle take care of the boy for him. However, he seethed at his lapse of attention that had allowed the kid to escape, shouting out curses that would make even a teenager blush. Being half Nicaraguan, Tadeo had the dark hair and dark skin of his mother, but he had the pale blue eyes of his father who was British. When he smiled, Tadeo was actually handsome and could be quite charming, but his anger turned his face into a picture only Shrek could appreciate.

He made his way quickly back to the clearing and the waiting helicopter. The pilot, as ill-tempered as the man who had hired him, angrily gestured at Tadeo to retrieve his belongings from the helicopter; he had another job and wanted to get back.

Tadeo ran over and gathered up the two bags, only just jumping back in time as the impatient man lifted off the ground. He began walking, then thought to himself: there was no need for him to take the bag he had collected from the airport; just the package inside. He tossed his own bag beside him on the grass and focused on his nephew's holdall. At least the bag had made it. Tadeo paused for a moment thoughtfully. What if Benito and not managed to put the package in like he had instructed? What if it had been found by security? No, if Benito had put it in, it would still be there. Security would have confiscated the whole bag – and his nephew – if the package had been found. He paused, then suddenly, opened the zip forcefully and pulled everything out so he could feel along the bottom and find the box. Taking a knife from his jacket pocket, Tadeo slit the bottom and slipped his hand underneath the lining.

A smile turned his face attractive again and he pulled out the thin titanium box. With the tip of the knife, he pried it open, his smile widening slowly, counting. Suddenly his face turned red with rage. There were some missing!

"That scoundrel of a nephew!" Tadeo shouted out loud in his anger. "He'll pay for all the trouble he has caused me." Tadeo muttered, closing up the box and his knife, and slipping them both into his jacket pocket, zipped it up securely. He hesitated a moment before scooping up the contents of the bag and shoving them back inside. With one smooth movement, he threw his bag over his shoulder and his nephew's into a bush.

Tadeo looked at the sun, low on the horizon; he would have to go quickly if he was going to make it to the little village before dark.

Toby stood, stretching his legs that had begun to ache from his exertion. He took a step and stopped. A prayer might be a good idea just now. His parents and his older brother Joe, probably would have been praying hours ago. Toby used to talk to God, but over the last few years he had slowly stopped believing there was Anyone there to hear. After all, hadn't evolution and other scientific facts proved there was no God? He paused for a moment, thoughts whirling around his head. Toby took a deep breath.

"Well, God," he breathed out slowly through pursed lips, "If You ARE there, I could really use Your help right now."

Short, but heartfelt prayer voiced, Toby headed back in the direction from which he had come.

CHAPTER 2

MONDAY 2nd July – Canada

The tall, grey-haired woman held open her slender arms to greet her "nephew". Her bright blue eyes and near permanent smile made her appear much younger than her sixty-one years.

The boy's nervous black eyes darted searchingly around the near-empty reception area and his face lit up as Doreen called out,

"Tobias!" She greeted him with an unexpectedly firm embrace.

"Toby, Aunty Doreen," Benito returned her smile, "I prefer Toby."

"Yes, yes, so your mother told me! What took you so long?"

"I had trouble finding my bag." He looked down at the green suitcase. He had had to wait until most of the bags had been claimed before he could try to find the bag that had stickers matching the ones on Toby's plane ticket. Doreen shook her head, still smiling.

"Just as well. You've grown up so much since I last saw you; almost a man!" She tipped her head slightly and smiled crookedly. "I might not have recognised you if you had come out with everyone else." The bubbly woman gave him another hug. "Well, grab your suitcase and come on. Uncle Derrick is waiting in the car. His leg is still quite painful when he stands for too long so I told him to wait there. He'll be wondering where we are." As if on cue, Elvis Presley's smooth voice rang out loudly from her purse and Doreen grabbed her mobile phone just as he started singing 'Let me be ... your Teddy Bear.'

"We're coming now, dear. Tobias – I mean Toby," she winked at Benito, "had trouble finding his bag." She paused as she listened to a response, and Benito's heart skipped a beat as he heard the question. Laughing, she answered, "No dear, he hasn't changed THAT much! Still that good looking boy that reminds me of you when you were young!" She laughed heartily and hung up without saying goodbye.

Doreen walked briskly through the door into the bright sunshine and Benito squinted. Doreen looked over at him and chortled as she kept up her stride.

"Not used to the sunshine, eh?" Benito could not help grinning back at this lively woman, whose personality seemed to reflect the sunshine that permeated the sky. "Your Uncle Derrick and I have never once regretted moving here from Liverpool. Lovely sunshine and lovely friends!" She paused as they entered the parking area. "Now, where on earth did we park?" She chuckled and gave the boy a nudge with her elbow. "Maybe we'll have to wait till the parking lot empties a bit and then we can find the car!"

Before Benito could reply, a voice called out, "Doreen!"

Doreen and Benito turned to their right, in the direction from which the voice came.

"Derrick! What on earth are you doing? I thought I told you to wait in the car!"

The boy followed her gaze and saw a tall, well built man with a shaved head, about sixty, Benito guessed, breathing heavily as he struggled along on crutches with a leg cast. The man stopped as Doreen called out to him.

"Well, Honey," he said slowly and firmly, "I figured you would probably forget where we parked and this was easier than trying to explain over the phone."

"You have no faith in me," she pouted playfully.

He tilted his head. "Obviously my lack of faith has been substantiated, since you were headed in the wrong direction."

Doreen winked at Benito again. "Now, now, dear, we were just going to head down this way, weren't we, Toby?"

Benito looked from one face to the other, quickly warming to this friendly couple. He hesitated before saying tactfully, "Well, I certainly did not know where I was going. I was just following," he touched the woman's arm gently, "my lovely Aunty Doreen, whom I am sure had every intention of turning into the direction from which you have just come!"

The big man just shook his head gently and pulled Benito into a loving embrace as they approached. He wobbled slightly as he let go of his crutches and Benito panicked as he thought he might have to stop Derrick from falling, but the man quickly steadied himself and the three headed slowly through the parked cars until finally stopping by an immaculate midnight blue '69 Mustang convertible.

"Wow! Nice car!" Benito stroked it gently with awe. What an amazing car; and what an amazing couple!

Derrick looked at him quizzically, and Benito started, realizing at once that he must have said something to give himself away. "Why so surprised? We e-mailed you all a picture when we bought it last month."

Benito's heart raced as he searched quickly for a convincing reply. "Oh … well," he sputtered, "it just … looks so much more impressive in real life!" He chanced a glance in the man's piercing brown eyes and saw his puzzled face break into a pleased smile.

"Ya, she's a beauty all right!" He slapped Benito on the back in a friendly manner, and Benito turned quickly to make sure Derrick had not unbalanced himself again. However, the jovial man was hanging onto the door of the car. "Sling your suitcase in back, son, and climb in. Strap up, your Aunt Doreen is a crazy driver!"

Doreen scowled as she climbed in the driver's seat. "It's the law, anyway, sweetheart!"

"What? That you have to use a seatbelt; or that you have to drive crazy?"

Benito felt himself being drawn into the couple's frivolity as Doreen paid for the parking and sped down the road – well, with the teasing and the wind blowing in his hair, it *felt* like she was driving fast. However, when Benito gathered the courage to surreptitiously check the speedometer, he noted they were actually 10 km/h below the speed limit. He tittered to himself. With the wind making conversation virtually impossible, and lost in the pleasure of having outsmarted his terrifying uncle, he leaned back to enjoy the ride.

———⟫●⟪———

Just when Toby was beginning to feel desperate, thinking that he had gone the wrong way, the small clearing appeared before him. The peacefulness was a stark contrast to the earlier cacophony from which he had escaped and Toby sighed deeply, relaxing the muscles he had not realized were tense.

The clearing was slightly oval shaped and only just big enough for the helicopter to land; the pilot must be very skilful. As Toby's gaze ran quickly over the clearing, a small flash of red caught his eye.

Curious, Toby walked across the long grass toward some ferns that lined the far side of the clearing. Tucked underneath the leaves was the holdall they had collected from the baggage claim. The contents had obviously been pulled out and stuffed unceremoniously back in so that it could not be zipped up.

Perhaps there would be a clue as to what was going on, thought Toby; or at the very least, a bit of food. He knelt down and started slowly removing the contents. Absently, he swatted at a mosquito.

Most of the things were items of clothing. He put on a baseball cap and then picked up a bandana – people in jungle movies often wore bandanas, so it must be useful, mused Toby, half laughing to himself.

"Ah!" He said out loud as his hand hit something hard. A Swiss army knife. "That would surely be an asset in the jungle." He shoved it into a deep pocket in his cargo shorts, swatting another mosquito on his leg as he withdrew his hand.

"This looks promising!" He said quietly as he hooked out a plastic bag. Opening it up, he felt like a kid at Christmas, and he was not disappointed. Three bottles of Vimto – not his favourite drink, but certainly welcome! – a huge bag of mixed, salted nuts, a couple of bags of Mr Porky's pork scratchings, two large packs of McVities plain chocolate digestives (best not to open them in this heat!) and a huge bar of Galaxy chocolate that felt pretty much like soup. It was a good job it was in completely sealed packaging.

There was not much else that interested Toby except a couple of items of clothing – jeans and a sweatshirt in case it got cold; and a bottle of mosquito repellent – that would *definitely* be useful! He opened the bottle and sprayed himself all over.

He started to put the unwanted items back in when he noticed a slit in the material at the bottom. Had there been something hidden there, he wondered? Even though Toby assumed the mystery item had been located and taken, he found himself reaching in the slit and feeling around. His impulsiveness was quickly rewarded when his fingers touched a folded piece of paper.

Unfolding it excitedly, he found a hand drawn map with what looked like trees, rivers and various symbols. It was drawn with a rather childlike hand, but Toby finally concluded that the smaller of the two X's scrawled on the sheet was probably the meadow where he was standing. The other X had 'Uncle's hideout' scribbled beside it, and halfway between the X's and to the right, was a badly drawn skull and crossbones. The fluttering butterflies inside his stomach grew frantic – it looked like there was more than Uncle Tadeo to worry about. As if *he* was not enough!

Toby bit his bottom lip pensively. He did not really feel inclined to head in the direction of madman Tadeo's hideout, but Toby did not know the way back to civilization on his own. He sighed contemplatively. Maybe he could spy on them and get some kind of information to help him find a way out. He did not have a whole lot of choice.

Standing up and stretching all his limbs, he glanced down at the map again to see if there was anything else of which he should take note. What was that splodgy round orange and black symbol with – Toby squinted – five dashes coming from it?

A soft, low rumble interrupted his thoughts and he looked up. Toby stopped breathing. A huge, beautiful jaguar was just sauntering out of the jungle towards the river. Toby was caught between terror and awe as he gazed motionless at the magnificent creature. Toby's knees started to buckle and it took all of his strength to keep upright and not draw the animal's attention. The topaz eyes were intently focused ahead as it slowed down and stopped at the river's edge. Time stood still as Toby waited, his heart pounding heavily against his rib cage. Several minutes passed as the jaguar stood silently surveying the area across the water thoughtfully.

Toby stood watching, not daring to make a sound or move a muscle; his body began to ache at the effort, yet he was paralysed with fear. Questions raced round his head. Would the animal see him? Would it turn and attack? Toby's eyes – the only thing in his body that moved – glanced across the river in the direction the jaguar was gazing. A little herd of small, reddish-brown deer with white bottoms were unsuspectingly grazing, oblivious to the impending danger. The slight breeze was blowing towards the jaguar and him, and the deer were intently feeding with their backs turned. Toby guessed they had recently been to the river to drink as he could just make out fresh hoof prints on the slightly sandy bank.

Finally, the jaguar began to slowly inch forward, the movement barely visible, and several more minutes ticked by. Finally the creature entered the water and quietly waded into the middle where he swam expertly and quietly, the babbling of the gentle river just masking any noise the animal made as he crawled stealthily out the other side, the water dripping silently off of him. The grass was a couple of feet tall and the jaguar crouched down until Toby could barely see him. Toby held his breath and waited, his eyes glued to the nearly invisible camouflaged head. The only thing moving were his delicate ears as they slowly turned back and forth, taking in the surrounding sounds while his eyes were locked onto a young deer, standing slightly away from the rest of the group. It was only a baby. Toby wanted to shout and warn the animal of its imminent fate, but decided it was better for the young animal to be the jaguar's dinner than him. Besides, Toby doubted he could make a noise if he wanted to.

Suddenly, the big cat leaped up and grabbed the deer by the neck with its massive teeth, easily pulling it to the ground with one swift movement. The other deer suddenly realized the danger, and, ignoring the poor little victim, bounded away as if they were one being.

"Wow!" Toby thought. He could think of no words that accurately described his awe. How many times had he seen that kind of thing on nature programs, but to see it in real life … "Wow!" The paralysis seeped out of his body and he sank to the ground in a heap, exhausted at his efforts to remain invisible. His respiration had just returned to normal when he looked up to see the jaguar swimming back across the river, his dinner firmly in his great jaws. Self-preservation took over and once again he became inert, watching the jaguar's effortless movements as he reached the shore and dragged his prey along the grass, moving more quickly than he had on the outward journey. Reaching a tree, the animal hefted up the deer and slowly climbed to one of the outstretched branches where it expertly slung its dinner securely before hungrily tucking in.

Toby sat watching for a moment, then, looking down at his map that was still clenched in his hands, he slowly rose to his feet and headed south along the river bank.

CHAPTER 3

Canada

Benito smiled with pleasure as Doreen slowed the car and turned up a long, steep drive and stopped at a large, sky blue house with a white veranda that ran along the front and to one side. It was built into the hill so that the front was two stories and at the back, it looked like a bungalow. The large, tidy garden was full of colour from various flowers and shrubs, and two large trees, a birch and a maple, stood like sentries on opposite corners, their shadows giving much-needed relief from the scorching sun. Benito instantly decided that he was going to enjoy his vacation here.

Doreen led the way into the house, and down some stairs to show Benito where he would be staying. "You settle yourself in, and I'll go up and check on supper!" Doreen gave him another gentle hug and a wide smile before leaving the room.

Benito sat on the double bed in the cool basement bedroom, and gathered his thoughts before heading back upstairs, following the delicious smell of supper which was wafting through the doorway. He hoped he would be able to spend the entire summer here and just go back to England on Toby's return flight, but he sensed that Toby's Aunt and Uncle were shrewd people, so he would have to be continually on his guard if he wanted to stay here until then. His thoughts drifted to Toby. By now he would be in the jungle, walking to – if not already at – the hideout with Benito's Uncle Tadeo. Benito felt guilty about having tricked Toby, but he seemed like a smart kid. Toby would surely be able to handle himself. Besides, Benito was a coward, plain and simple, and his cowardice outweighed his guilt. When he met Toby at the airport, the idea had just came to him all at once, like an unexpected gift. He sent his uncle a text saying there had been 'complications' and someone else would be arriving in Managua with the package. It had seemed the perfect solution to his dilemma. His uncle had wanted him to get more and more involved, and Benito had been terrified about being a courier for him.

Benito had spent many holidays with his uncle while his mom, a single parent, had had to work. Tadeo was a cruel, manipulative man, and although Benito had tried to tell his mom why he did not want to spend any more time with him, she did not believe her beloved little brother could be evil and thought Benito was lying so he could stay home when she worked. But Benito had sat with his uncle in dark alleys, waiting for men who would swap money for guns; then worry about the man who had provided the guns sending someone to finish off his uncle for swindling him out of money. That hadn't happened yet, but he had lain awake many a night worrying. Once, Benito himself was sent with a gun to a man in a hotel room – no one would suspect a boy, his uncle had said. Benito had been scared, but he had been even more scared of refusing his uncle who was not hesitant to use his fist on him.

A few times, Benito had watched as his uncle roughed up men when Tadeo himself had been swindled. And once, his uncle had even killed a man. It had been a terrifying ordeal. Benito could still see the man, shot through the heart, crumple in a heap on the warehouse floor, blood trickling through his fingers as he clenched his chest. It was a horrific image that would never leave him.

Benito shook himself and headed up the stairs. He needed to escape his thoughts, and the warm couple upstairs were just the thing to help him.

Doreen gave him a huge smile and a warm hug as Benito entered the kitchen. "I am SO pleased you volunteered to come and help us! Actually, I am just pleased to see you again! It has been far too long! One downfall of moving so far away, is not seeing family so often." Her smile faded slightly as she looked at him. "I guess there are ONE or two regrets moving here, after all." She paused before brightening animatedly, "But you are here now, so let's enjoy the time we have together!" She motioned to one of six chairs that faced a large oak table.

"Sit down, Toby! I hope you enjoy supper; your mom told me your favourite meal, so I hope you find my version as delicious as your mom's." She giggled like a schoolgirl. "Actually, it SHOULD be, since we both have the same recipe from her mom, my sister!"

Benito smiled as Doreen put a huge plate of lasagne in front of him. He grabbed his fork, then realized that Derrick and Doreen both had their heads bowed and Derrick began speaking. Benito quietly put the down the fork and bowed his head as well while Derrick said grace, then they all tucked in.

This was going to be the best summer ever!

———⟫●⟪———

Toby walked quickly at first, but soon found the sweat dripping off of him. He paused for a moment and crouched down beside the river he was following to take a drink. He cupped his hands and brought the welcome liquid to his lips, then splashed some more on his face and neck, enjoying the cooling sensation on his burning skin. As he did, his eye caught something moving slowly on the other side, just below the surface of the water; something very large. Suddenly, it came near enough to the surface to see its full shape. A crocodile! Toby stared for a moment, watching the gentle rippling of the water in the otherwise calm pool where the river widened enough to slow down to an imperceptible flow. Mesmerized by the proximity of such a dangerous creature that he had only before seen in a zoo, Toby sat down, only to jump immediately to his feet as the ripple turned and headed towards him. He trotted on, not looking back and hoping the beast would not want to leave his comfortable position below the surface of the water.

The shadows lengthened quickly and Toby looked up towards the west. The sun was setting awfully fast. Of course! It would set faster nearer the equator. He had not thought of that. He would never make it to the hideout before dark. Panicking, his eyes darted around, desperately looking for somewhere to spend the night. Although leopards could climb trees, Toby had an inkling that there were many more unsavoury characters that would lurk on the ground in the night; besides, the nearest jaguar had just caught and eaten his dinner; he would surely no longer be hungry for the evening! Spotting a tree that had several large, reasonably high and somewhat level, branches close together, he trotted over and jumped up to the lowest branch. They had a couple of large trees in his back garden at home, and he and Joe used to have competitions to see who could climb fastest, so although he tired quickly – it had been a while! – he climbed expertly up several branches until he reached the group that would serve as his bed for the night.

As Toby tried to make the branches more comfortable by breaking off leafy twigs from around him and laying them down, he wondered if he would be able to sleep on such an uncomfortable bed. Before he was finished, an inky darkness had settled around him. He would have to plan better tomorrow. Tomorrow. The next day. How long would it take to get back home, or to his aunt and uncle's place. *Would* he get back home?

He put on the sweatshirt and lay down on his makeshift bed. Looking up, he could just see a small gap in the canopy where several stars were silently twinkling. Somehow, the familiarity of the lights comforted him, and he soon relaxed. Exhaustion from the day quickly overpowered him, and within a few minutes, Toby was asleep.

CHAPTER 4

Toby's eyes jerked open. A loud sharp bark and high pitched squeaking had snatched him from his dreams and back onto his nest in the trees. His heart pounded at his ribs and several seconds went by before he could remember where he was. Toby's ears were ringing from the blood pulsating through him, and he struggled to stop hyperventilating. He was surrounded by … things. Paralyzed by fear, his eyes started taking in small shapes scattered around him on the branches. Something furry touched his hand and Toby screamed, sending all the shapes scurrying through the branches, squeaking and barking, and the pandemonium was deafening. In the distance, he heard a roar – the jaguar? Toby strained to see around him, automatically gathering himself into a fetal position to protect himself from the alarming black figures that continued to dart back and forth across the branches.

Something flew past his face, and goosebumps raced across his body. Then another flew past. And another. He felt a little scratch on his hand as a creature landed lightly. He started flailing about as more small fluttering beings flew past or tried to land on him. The small leafy branches that had made up his bed were flung in the air in Toby's panic to rid himself of the swarm of … what? Just then, he caught the silhouette of one of his attackers – a bat! He jumped up, forgetting he was in a tree, and his legs slipped through the branches. Pain cursed through his body as he bounced down towards the ground, ricocheting off the branches as he fell. Toby grasped wildly and at the last branch, he managed to grab hold and stopped himself with a jerk.

"Oomph!" Toby's breath was sucked out of him as the unforgiving branch punched his stomach. Several slow seconds past before oxygen finally made its way back into his straining lungs. Taking multiple, deep laboured breaths, he lay draped over the branch, listening to the strange callings in the night; waiting ... waiting. Finally, enough strength seeped back into his muscles to pull himself up onto the branch in a more comfortable position. He crawled cautiously across the branch towards the trunk so he could have some support until he could recover from his painful descent.

The roaring intermittently interrupted the squeaks and the barks and the insects buzzing in the warm night air. There were so many different sounds that all melded together like the myriad of instruments in an orchestra that were each practising before the beginning of a concert. Trumpets, tubas, flutes, clarinets, violins, oboes. Squeaking, twanging, honking, tweeting, trilling. Loud and shrill and soft and gentle. Then, slowly, he was drawn in to the symphony and the chaos gradually grew together into a soft beautiful harmony that almost lulled Toby back to sleep.

Nearly an hour passed when Toby decided he could manage to drag himself slowly back up to where he had been sleeping. When he finally reached his spot, he groped around for a few minutes before his hand finally found his backpack. Toby zipped open the bag and found the bottle. Clumsily, he opened the drink and downed the welcome liquid.

Toby rested against the trunk wearily, then realized the small shapes were still there, moving around restlessly. The barking and squeaking began again – or had it ever stopped? Again he heard the roaring; this time much closer! What was that? What were those shapes? The calming effect of the noise earlier now changed to a gradual fear creeping into Toby's tense body as his imagination ran wild as to what was surrounding him.

Sweat dripped down his face from the muggy air, the exertion – and the fear, as the creatures, continuing in their raucous chatter, seemed to be closing in on him. He covered his ears and squeezed his eyes shut, whispering,

"Please God, help me! Please God, help me!" He repeated over and over. The noise lessened and the pounding in his ears began to relent in time with the slow calming of his heart rate. Toby could still see the shapes in the branches, as they began settling down. Finally he recognised the shapes – monkeys! Their chattering squeaks became more gentle, but the roaring in the background continued. He jumped as a tiny hand rested on his arm, but the noise the monkey made almost sounded like it was trying to comfort him, and he relaxed slightly, though remaining hunched up like a frightened child. The rest of the troop appeared to settle down on the branches, but the one little monkey seemed to sense his need for consolation and began stroking Toby's cheek with the backs of his little fingers. A smile curled the corners of Toby's mouth despite his remaining apprehension, and unconsciously he relaxed his tightly curled position, lowering his legs and arms a little bit. It was only a small movement, but it was enough to allow the little monkey space to crawl into his lap and snuggle in. Slowly, eventually, somehow, Toby drifted off to sleep.

⸺⸎⸻

Benito sighed contentedly as he placed his fork on the empty plate. Derrick and Doreen were only half finished their meals, and Doreen smiled widely.

"I guess you were hungry!"

"I sure was!" answered Benito heartily. "You know what aeroplane food is like. Well, how little you get, I mean!" He exhaled loudly through his nose. "That, Aunty Doreen, was absolutely delicious! I do not remember tasting anything so good as that for, well, a long time!"

"I would not have thought it was that much different to the way your mom makes it," Doreen half laughed, looking slightly bemused, "But I appreciate your enthusiasm!"

Benito silently reprimanded himself for his error. It was going to be tougher than he thought to keep up the facade.

"I thought we would Skype your parents tomorrow morning," Doreen interrupted his thoughts. "They'll want to hear about your first journey on your own!"

Benito's jaw dropped slightly for a second, before he tried to pull his mouth into a smile, grasping desperately for something sensible to say. Derrick and Doreen were looking at him questioningly. Recovering, he sputtered,

"You know, I AM nearly eighteen. I don't need to stay in touch with my parents continually. You remember what it is like to be my age, don't you?" He tried to produce a cocky smirk, but he sensed Derrick was not entirely convinced by his act. Doreen's trusting nature intervened on his behalf.

"I remember quite well," Doreen responded. "However! I also can imagine what it is like to be the mother of a seventeen year old!" Benito remembered Toby explaining that Derrick and Doreen had never been able to have children.

Picking up Benito's plate, Doreen stood and walked over to the counter where an amazing chocolate cake sat. Placing a huge slice on a plate, she walked back over and handed it to him.

"So, first thing tomorrow, we Skype!" She said determinedly.

Benito faked a submissive smile, and pretended to focus his attention on the delicious cake, which now tasted like chalk in his dry mouth, while Doreen chattered away about what they would do while he was with them. She seemed to forget that he had come to help them settle in to their new home.

Finally, Benito pushed his chair away from the table. "I don't feel very well, I think I ate too much. " He stood up, stretching and yawning. "I suddenly feel quite tired. Do you mind if I head to bed?" Over his right shoulder, a large clock on the wall caught his eye. It was only eight o'clock. Underneath the clock was a desk with a computer; presumably the one they would Skype on the next day. His shoulders sagged with defeat, but Derrick interpreted the motion as fatigue.

"You get on to bed, son" he said kindly. "You've had a long day."

Benito started out of the kitchen, then paused. He turned around and gave each of them a grateful hug, the warmth of their return embraces touching his heart.

"Thank you," he said with heartfelt emotion, swallowing the lump in his throat. "Thanks for a lovely meal and, well, in advance for an enjoyable summer." He smiled faintly and this time continued out of the kitchen, across the living room and down to the welcome relief of his bedroom.

Wearily, he stripped down to his boxers and climbed under the cool fresh sheets. The bed felt like heaven, but thoughts of Skyping Toby's parents the next day plagued him, preventing him from drifting off to a sleep that his body so craved. A picture of the computer glared at him in his mind. Suddenly the picture became clearer, and he saw something beside the computer. Lying on the desk had been a small roll of invisible tape.

"I wonder … " he said softly to himself. Crawling out of bed, he dug in his bag for his phone and set an alarm for midnight. Having sorted a possible solution to his problem, he finally relaxed, and this time, when he lay back down, he was asleep before his head hit the pillow.

A few hours later, a soft beep gently brought Benito back to consciousness and he shook the fog from his brain trying to remember where he was and why his phone was waking him in the middle of the night. Slowly, he remembered the plan that had formed in his mind last night, and he threw back the duvet. Nervously, he crept out of his room, and moved silently up the carpeted stairs into the kitchen. Fortunately, the moon was bright, and he could see the computer and tape clearly. He opened one of the drawers, hoping for luck to be on his side, and was rewarded quickly – a pair of scissors! He held his breath as he picked up the roll and cut off a small piece. Wonderful! They were very sharp and made a clean edge as he slowly cut a small circle. Very carefully, he took the tiny circle of tape and pressed it firmly over the webcam.

Benito froze on the spot. He heard a noise from the bedroom just off the kitchen. Someone was getting up! He did not dare move, hoping against hope that Derrick or Doreen would just go to their ensuite and not come out into the kitchen. He heard the knob turn and Benito panicked. Hearing the sound of Derrick hobbling along on his crutches, Benito quickly opened the drawer and threw the scissors in, shutting it just as the kitchen light switched on.

It would have been easier if it had been Doreen. Startled, Derrick stepped back with his healthy foot, nearly falling backwards, as he saw Benito standing in front of the computer.

"Uh, I was looking for a glass to get some water and I … uh … lost my way in the kitchen!" stumbled Benito. Hopefully, Derrick would have been too sleepy to notice how bright it had been in the kitchen before he switched on the light.

Derrick smiled and narrowed his eyes, looking at Benito gently. "Easy to get disorientated in the middle of the night in a strange house," he responded graciously. He made his way to a cupboard to the right of the sink. Leaning on the crutches with his arms, he opened it up, taking down a tall glass and handing it to Benito. "If you like it cold, there is water from the fridge." He pointed to the dispenser on the front of the large appliance. Benito walked over to it and fumbled with the lever, filling the glass full, thankful to have his back to Derrick while he composed himself.

"Thanks!" he turned to Derrick and smiled. Turning, Benito walked slowly out of the kitchen, though every muscle in his body wanted to run.

Back in the safety of the bedroom, Benito sat on the edge of the bed and drank the water, finding he actually was quite thirsty. He placed the empty glass on the drawers beside him and lay back down. A few minutes later, his breathing had returned to normal and he drifted back off to sleep.

———⇒●⇐———

TUESDAY 3rd July

A soft knock on his door roused him and Benito opened his eyes. It seemed awfully bright.

"Yes?" he called out sleepily. Doreen poked her head around the door and smiled brightly at him. Benito suddenly realized the second part of his plan and added in a raspy voice "Come in."

"I was just checking you were still alive!" she chirped. "Are you ok? You sound a little croaky."

"I'm all right, just a little hoarse from the dry air, I think. Not used to it! What time is it?"

"Nearly eleven thirty! Half the day is gone! Would you like some porridge? Derrick and I ate ages ago and are nearly ready for lunch!"

"Sorry," Benito grimaced as he sat up and his head started pounding. "Oh!" he held his head in his hands and Doreen instantly rushed over to him and put a comforting hand on his shoulder, concerned.

"What is the matter?"

Benito warmed in her caring gaze, and a pang saddened him as he thought of his own mother who, even though very tired from her long hours at the factory, had always managed to give him a smile and a hug when she walked through the door. Laying back down, he smiled feebly up at Doreen. He got lots of headaches. They did not last long, but the pain seared through to the middle of his brain and he squinted. He could not explain to his doctor about his uncle and the terrible worry he suffered when he was staying with him, so the doctor had just put his headaches down to adolescent changes and prescribed him some painkillers to take as and when he needed them.

"I just have a headache – I get them sometimes. I have some painkillers in my backpack."

Doreen moved towards the bag, and alarmed, Benito hoarsely called out a little louder than necessary, "No! That's OK!"

Doreen, puzzled at the sharpness in his tone, moved away from him, taking a step back towards the door.

"I'm sorry, I didn't mean to sound rude. I can't take them on an empty stomach," he said, smiling weakly, trying to make amends for his abruptness. "I'll bring one up with me when I come, and take it after I have had something to eat."

"Would you like some porridge or toast?" she asked softly.

"A couple of pieces of toast would be just fine." Then added quickly, "Thanks so much, Aunty Doreen, you are a treasure!" She smiled faintly, pacified by his softly spoken praise, and shut the door.

That was close, thought Benito. If she had taken the bottle out of his bag and looked at it, it would have been extremely difficult to explain his name, Benito, on the prescription. Trying not to move too quickly, he gingerly got out of bed and put on his clothes from the day before, trying to move his head as little as possible. He was not up to searching through Toby's bag to find something fresh to wear.

Reaching in his own backpack, he found the inside pocket and took out two bottles. He looked at the labels, and put the sleeping tablets back. His uncle had gotten those for him, from a doctor friend. Not only did he get terrible headaches, but the stress when he was with his uncle made it nearly impossible for him to sleep. He had tried getting something from his own doctor to help him sleep, but Dr Lawden would only give him the painkillers – and those only because he could have bought them from a chemist anyway.

The sleeping tablets had come in handy at the airport. It was fortunate for him that, just before they had to go to the departure gates, Toby asked him to watch his bag while he went to the toilet, handing over his can of Pepsi as well. He had been gone just long enough for Benito to swap the passport and ticket, and pop a few of the sleeping tablets in the drink. That way, Toby would be too groggy to realize he was on the wrong plane. Fortunately too, their departure gates were close together, and his flight left twenty minutes before Toby's. He had managed to keep Toby occupied until just before the plane took off, so that when Toby tried to get through the gate to Calgary, he would be rushed over to the other gate and there would be no time for questions. Once Toby had been hurriedly guided through onto the other plane, Benito had just casually picked up his own backpack, and gone through the last check, and onto the plane to a hopefully pleasant summer, instead of danger of an unknown quantity in a Nicaraguan jungle. It had all worked out perfectly ... so far.

The pain in his head brought him back to the present. Placing two painkillers in the palm of his hand, he screwed the cap back on and popped that bottle back in the bag pocket and zipped it shut.

As he turned to leave, he caught sight of his mobile on the cupboard by the bed. He had had just enough power the previous night to send his uncle a message and set the alarm. It probably had little to no power left now. He should get a Canadian adapter so he could charge it. Then he smiled thoughtfully. There was no rush, was there?

Then carefully, Benito climbed the stairs and into the kitchen where various jars of jams and peanut butter lay beside several slices of toast on the table. Doreen placed a large glass of orange juice in front of him as he sat down. He picked up a piece of toast and Doreen chided him, motherly.

"Don't forget to say grace, dear." Benito panicked. He had no idea what to say. He had never prayed before. He bowed his head and pretend to pray quietly to himself for a moment, then opened his eyes and started on his breakfast.

Slowly, he ate his toast in silence, his head still pounding, then popped the tablets in his mouth and downed his juice thirstily. He took a breath and smiled up at Doreen as she sat down opposite him with a cup of coffee in a large bright orange mug with big yellow flowers all over it. It suited her perfectly.

"How is your head?" She asked, gently patting him on the hand, then squeezed it caringly.

"A little better, actually," he said in a weak voice, rubbing his temples. "And the tablets will start working quickly to clear it completely."

"How about a cup of tea?" Doreen got up and went over to the cupboard before Benito answered, taking down a smaller, plain beige mug. "What kind would you like?"

"Just plain ordinary tea, thanks, with a large splash of milk." Within seconds, the tea was in front of him, and they both drank slowly; Benito gladly listening in silence as Doreen, slightly less animatedly than usual, chattered on about the things she wanted Benito to help her with in the garden. With any luck, thought Benito, she would forget about the Skyping.

Within minutes of that thought, the door that lead out onto the deck opened up and Derrick hobbled in, stopping Doreen mid flow in her description of the compost bin she wanted Benito to help her build.

"Hello, sweetheart," she beamed at him as she stood and took out another cup, filling it from the coffee pot on the side and placing it down on a mat.

Derrick leaned the crutches against the side of the table and lowered himself carefully onto the big wooden chair, holding the arms firmly, and picked up the coffee, gratefully taking a few sips before he spoke.

"I am afraid that deck needs staining after all." He paused, before adding, "I am beginning to think we may have to hire some help as well. There is just too much for Toby to do on his own."

Turning suddenly to Benito, he said, "We ought to be Skyping soon, otherwise it will be too late for your parents! I think they go to bed, early, don't they?"

Benito just smiled lamely, wondering if Doreen and Derrick could hear his heart pounding. He looked at the computer and realized he was awfully close. Too close. Picking up his dishes, he put them into the dishwasher and surreptitiously sat down in a different chair, farther away and at a slight angle to the computer that sat staring at him accusingly. Doreen switched on the machine and turned to her husband.

"I just click on this icon thingy, right?" Derrick rolled his eyes, but replied in a patient voice.

"Yes, dear, it is all ready set up and good to go. Do you want to give your niece a quick call to make sure they have theirs turned on?"

"No, Emily said she would leave it on and have the volume turned up so she would hear us call." Doreen tapped at the keyboard and within a couple of minutes, Emily's smiling face was on the screen. Benito was surprised at the similarity: Emily was a younger version of her aunt.

"Hey there Tobs, Dad has a very early start tomorrow, so he went to bed half an hour ago, he said to give you a big kiss" she kissed her palm and blew at the screen. "How was your first trip on your own?" Benito felt his face grow warm as he cleared his throat, and swallowed before responding in a raspy voice.

"Uh ... ya, it was OK. " He self consciously put one hand up to his face, trying to be inconspicuous but feeling completely exposed.

"Are you all right? You sound funny – and everything looks kind of foggy there!" She squinted at the screen.

"Uh ... ya ... I woke up with a sore throat," he croaked, "must be the dry air. I feel fine, though ... Mom."

"You did have a headache as well earlier, though, didn't you honey?" Doreen piped up, adding "That is strange, Emily, I can't imagine why we look foggy. Maybe something is wrong with the computer."

"You don't normally get headaches, are you sure you are OK, sweetie?" Emily's face looked concerned as she continued squinting. Pressing some buttons, she continued, "I can't seem to adjust anything here to get you clearer – it must be your end, Aunt Dor." Derrick started to stand, and Doreen put a hand on his shoulder,

"Don't worry Derrick, you sit down. I'll see what I can do."

Derrick snorted. "Darling, what on *earth* do you think *you* are going to do? You can barely turn the thing on!" She turned and scowled at him playfully, opening her mouth to speak.

"I'm fine, honestly," interrupted Benito, rubbing his one temple, "The headache is only on one side now." He continued, hoping the fogginess of the screen would be forgotten. "The trip was quick, 'cause I slept most of the way. " He remembered his conversation with Toby and added, "and no one abducted me!"

Emily smiled at what she thought was her son, "That is because you were careful, and watched out like I told you to!" Benito shook his head, and winced as the action triggered a stabbing pain.

"I may be a little on the slim slide, but I *am* nearly six foot tall; who is going to abduct me, Mom?" He was almost starting to enjoy himself.

"Are you sure your web cam doesn't need cleaning or something?"

Almost. Doreen grabbed the dishcloth from the sink and walked over. Suddenly Emily's face froze. "Oh dear, the signal dropped. We have been having trouble with the internet since we moved in. Can you still hear me, Em?"

"Yes, but you are cutting in and out. Maybe we should try tomorrow." Doreen's hand with the cloth dropped to her side, and Benito let out a quiet sigh of relief.

"Hmmm ... ya, probably a good idea."

"Bye Toby! Love you lots! Miss you already!"

"Bye Mom, I love you too." Benito said, then panicked, not knowing if that was something Toby would have said, and waited for any repercussion. Fortunately, none came. Derrick and Doreen said their goodbyes and switched off the computer.

"Well, that was unfortunate," said Doreen as she stood and walked over to the coffee machine to refill her cup. "Would you like some more, honey?"

Derrick shook his head, "No thanks." He then picked up the house phone and began dialling. "I'll get that engineer back today and see if he can't get the internet fixed so we can try again tomorrow."

CHAPTER 5

TUESDAY 3rd July – Nicaragua

Toby woke slowly, consciously becoming more aware of the warmth of a new day, and the aches that seemed to permeate every muscle in his body. As he wiped the perspiration from his forehead, he was sorry that he had put the sweatshirt on. He did not know if got cold at night in the jungle. Evidently not.

The fog in his mind cleared and he opened his eyes with a start as he heard a strange, but friendly chattering all around him. The monkeys were still there, this time happily eating some kind of fruit.

He turned his head sharply as something touched his shoulder. He smiled as he saw the little monkey from the previous night. She was holding a yellow fruit out to him. A mango, he suddenly realized. He took it from her gingerly, not wanting to frighten her. He laughed softly to himself at the reversal of attitude from the night before. She just sat there, watching him with a concern in her eyes that was almost human, and he was reminded of his mom. Taking a bite, his hunger immediately surfaced, and he hungrily took another bite. It was delicious! He quickly devoured the mango and threw the stone to the forest floor. The little monkey squeaked loudly and sprang into the air with apparent delight, disappearing through the leaves. A few moments later, she was back with another, which Toby consumed just as quickly. The monkey repeated her squeaks and again dashed off for another mango, which she presented eagerly to him. By the fourth mango, Toby ate more slowly. It probably was not good for his stomach to eat too much fresh fruit at once! Especially as he was not used to it.

"Thank you, little one." He reached out to the caring animal and she quickly jumped onto his shoulder and began scraping her little finger tips against his scalp.

"Ouch! Gentle!" he laughed as he realized she was grooming him. "I don't think I have any critters in my hair just yet!" The rest of the troop seemed to ignore him as they busied themselves grooming each other and keeping a watchful eye on a couple of youngsters who were messing around on a branch above him.

A few moments later, his grooming finished, the little monkey pounced on his lap and looked up at him, still seemingly concerned.

"You are just like my mom," Toby grinned, "I think I will name you Emmie, after her." He was not even sure that she *was* a 'she'. No, he thought to himself, he was sure. She had to be a girl. A boy would not have taken care of him the way she had. "What do you think of that? Do you like the name Emmie?" He stroked her head and she let out a sharp bark, jumping up and down. Toby burst out laughing. "Emmie it is, then."

Suddenly reality hit him. He was in the middle of who knew where and he had no idea why he was there or how he was going to get home. He shifted his position and cried out in agony at the pain in his rib. He hoped he hadn't broken anything. Emmie sprang to his shoulder and nuzzled his ear in concern.

"It's OK, Emmie," he groaned as he tried to get comfortable. "Well, I *think* it is OK. Maybe I will just sit here for a bit longer." He stretched out his arms and his legs slowly a few times and leaned back against the tree. Opening up his backpack, he dug down, searching for the bag of nuts. As he did he found a little black box and pulled it out. A Nintendo DS? What on earth? It must be Benito's, but why would he put it in his back pack? Oh well, his phone was out of charge, so he may as well see if this had any power. He could do with a bit of distraction. He opened the bag of nuts and popped a few in his mouth as he pressed the 'on' button.

Emmie had moved beside him, watching intently as he ate. He handed over a few nuts and she grabbed them eagerly. "It's the least I can do!" he said to her with a slight smile.

Turning back to his game and finding nothing had happened, he pushed the button again. Still nothing. Toby swore. It didn't even turn on. He smacked it with his hand a couple of times. Nothing. Hmmmpff ... so much for that. He lifted it above his head to sling it in disgust, and as he did so, he heard rattling inside. Maybe something was loose and he could fix it. He took out the knife and lifted up the screw driver head. In a few moments, he had the game open and he gasped. What ... ?!! They couldn't be! But then ... of course ... it kind of made sense ... sort of. He put the four pieces in the palm of his hand and raised them to the light. He'd put money on them being real. The light refracted into various beautiful colours as he stared amazed. Why were Benito and his uncle heading into the jungle with diamonds? His mind cast back to the cut in the bottom of the red bag. Benito's uncle must have been looking for the diamonds. Toby's heart sunk. That meant Toby probably had not seen the last of him. He closed his hand around the diamonds and turned to the little monkey sitting next to him, obliviously eating the nuts he had given her. "Why, Emmie? What's going on?" He bit his lip as he stared at her, so human-like that he almost expected her to answer. He had to get to the camp marked on the map. He had to find out what was going on. Sigh. He had to get home.

Toby gently put the diamonds back in the game and screwed on the cover. Something told him it was a good idea to keep them hidden, in the bottom of his bag. Gingerly, he put the bag over his shoulders and pulled himself to a standing position. Emmie jumped up and barked at him, as the rest of the monkeys barely took notice. He guessed they were used to him now and found him no threat.

Toby stretched out his limbs and, as pain raced through him, he let out another swear word and suddenly felt strangely convicted as little Emmie cocked her head at him. She almost looked reprovingly. "Sorry, Emmie, but I hurt. I hurt ALL over!" She tilted her head further and he smiled. "You're right. I won't say another bad word." With that, she opened her mouth and squeaked loudly, like she was laughing. "I mean it!" said Toby, starting to laugh himself, despite every inch of him throbbing. He bent down and very carefully, lowered himself to the next branch. It took so much effort, he had to wait for several minutes until he got his breath back.

And so it continued, branch by branch, waiting, breathing deeply, trying not to cry out with the agony that raged through him. He had to keep moving. He was convinced once he got to the ground, he would be able to walk and would feel better. Finally, he reached the bottom branch and there was nothing but forest floor below him. It seemed a lot farther than the distance between the branches he had just climbed down. Slowly, he crouched as low as possible, and grabbed the branch with both hands. As he did so, he jumped off backwards and let himself swing down and forward, intending to land gracefully, but the pain in his arms was so severe, he could not hang on and he fell in a crumpled heap, feeling certain he would never move again. Tears welled up as the pain intensified, and Toby shouted out to no one, "I am NOT going to cry!"

And immediately, the sobs came.

Toby heard a soft feminine voice before he became fully conscious, vaguely aware of someone wiping his face with a cool, damp cloth.

"Would you like a drink?"

"Mom?" his voice was raspy. No, it wasn't his mom's voice; and there was a slight accent he did not recognise. Why couldn't he open his eye lids? He took a deep breath and with all the effort he could muster, slowly opened his eyes, and as he did so he became aware that his wrists and ankles were tied. Tightly. But for some reason, the pain that had earlier racked his body, was somewhat dulled.

Opening his eyes, he saw a plain, but friendly face smiling down at him. The girl was about his age, with long, straight ebony hair and dark chocolate eyes. Her skin was olive and free from blemish making her look younger than she probably was.

"Did Tadeo and his men make all these bruises?" Her smile faded and she looked at him with the same concern that Emmie had. His eyes started to close.

"Uh … no," he breathed heavily, trying desperately to stay consciousness. What was wrong with him? "It was … a tree." Half her lip curled up in amusement.

"A tree?" Then realizing it would take Toby too much energy to explain, she changed the subject, handing him a cup with some cool liquid. "Here, drink this, it is coconut milk. It is full of vitamins and minerals and will make you feel better. It will also help protect against infections in your wounds."

"What about me? When do *I* get a drink? And please, no more of that stuff! Don't you people have any cordial or anything?" Toby turned at the posh English accent and through half open eyes, saw a girl, about his age, with wavy, shoulder length light blond hair, sitting in a fetal position on a mat on the opposite side of what looked like some kind of wooden hut with palm branches for a roof. Even with a dirty, tear-stained face, she was beautiful. Her marble green eyes flashed with a mix of fear and anger, and the dark haired girl spoke kindly to her.

"I will get you another drink shortly, Gwen, but I first need to help this boy. He looks like he has been through a severe beating."

Toby closed his eyes again, took another breath and opened them fully this time. The girl helped him to a sitting position and he took the cup in his bound hands and drank eagerly, feeling strength swim through his body as the liquid revived him.

"What happened?" he finally managed. Before the dark-haired girl could respond, she was interrupted by Gwen.

"When am I going home? I've been here for five days now and no one is telling me anything. My daddy will pay you anything you ask. Has anyone asked him yet? He and Mummy will be so worried. And Miss Sugar will be missing me terribly!" She paused for a quick breath and continued, "No one can give her the snuggles I do. She loves me to bits. Mummy and Daddy will be too worried to take her for proper walks." She finished her oration, her thoughts turning towards home, and her pampered Pekingese dog.

"I will let you know as soon as I have anything to tell you, Gwen, I promise." She turned back to Toby. "From what I can gather, you wouldn't tell them where Benito was," she answered him. They tried a truth drug on you, but before it took effect, you lost consciousness – probably from that big lump on your head. You are probably not feeling any pain now, though, right? That is another effect of the drug." He followed her gaze to his arms and legs, covered in scrapes and bruises. The blood had been washed off. Toby shook his head slightly, taking in what she had said. He did not remember anyone asking him about Benito. He did not remember anything. Perhaps it was a good thing.

"It is night now, Tadeo will not be back until tomorrow; he has gone hunting jaguar." She said grimly with a deep frown, and Toby felt a stab of compassion for the majestic animal he had seen the previous day. "There is much money to be made for such carcasses." She paused, thinking about the travesty, but as Gwen opened her mouth to speak, the girl continued, "My name is Rebeca, what is yours?"

"Toby." Finishing the last of the drink, he handed Rebeca the cup and started to lie back down. It was awkward with his limbs bound so securely. Rebeca put the cup on the floor and helped him get comfortable. He noticed Gwen was not bound. Presumably she was little threat, and almost certainly would not have tried to escape into the jungle by herself.

Refreshed but still sleepy, he closed his eyes and relinquished his fight against unconsciousness. Rebeca covered him with a blanket and left the hut to get Gwen a drink.

———————

TUESDAY 3rd July – Canada

Benito wiped his brow as he shoved the fork into the soil and took the lemonade from Doreen. Despite its frigid temperature, he drank the whole large glass in one long guzzle, handing the glass back to her with a big grin on his face. He wiped his mouth with the back of his dirty hand, smearing soil across his lips. "Thanks! That was delicious."

Benito looked over the twelve foot by twenty foot vegetable patch with satisfaction. It had taken him all afternoon, but he was nearly finished digging it. Another half an hour and he would be done. Doreen smiled back with pleasure.

"You have worked so hard, Toby, you must be starving! Supper will be ready in about forty-five minutes. I thought you might enjoy a nice big steak and baked potato." As if on cue, Benito's stomach rumbled loudly and they both laughed.

"Sounds great!"

Doreen turned and went back in the house, leaving Benito alone with his thoughts as he grabbed the fork and finished turning the soil. He was getting slower and slower as fatigue took over, but he had not felt so happy in a long time. How could Toby not have wanted to come? He could not have asked for friendlier hosts and he felt a small pang of conscience for his deception; but it quickly disappeared as his Uncle Tadeo's angry face flashed in his mind. His uncle was getting less and less tolerant of his cowardice and Benito was certain that he would have no qualms about hurting him ... or worse. Pushing thoughts of Toby's demise to the back of his mind, he carried on contentedly until he had finished his task.

He put his fork back in the little shed that stood at the corner of the patch. Striding tiredly to the back door, he turned right as he stepped in, to the bathroom where he washed the dirt off his face and hands thoroughly before drying them on the beige towel that Doreen had put out for him. Life was good here.

Despite his exhaustion, Benito almost floated across the living room floor as the tantalizing aroma of barbecued steak beckoned him into the kitchen. He was famished! He could probably eat a sixteen ounce steak plus all the trimmings. Benito gasped with delight as he sat down at the table and Doreen put the large steak before him. It was twice the size he had ever had before. The baked potato was large as well, and had been cut open and buttered. He smiled to his right at Derrick who sat at the head of the table.

"Wow!" was all he could say. Derrick smiled back.

"I do the barbecuing, and I cook a mean steak, if I do say so myself!" Doreen placed a large bowl of salad on the table between them and sat opposite Benito. Benito started to pick up his cutlery, but suddenly remembered the prayers, and bowed his head just as Derrick began to say grace.

During the meal, Derrick and Doreen discussed who they would get to deal with the large deck that ran around three quarters of the big bungalow, and Benito happily ate his food in silence, half listening, half thinking about the jobs that Doreen had written down on a list for him, and mentally putting them in order of difficulty. She had written down eight or nine tasks, like putting various items away on some high shelves downstairs in the store room, but the job he had done this afternoon was by far the most strenuous. The rest would be a breeze.

"Toby? What do you think?"

Forgetting for a moment his deception, Benito did not respond immediately to the name, still half thinking about the chores ahead of him.

"Toby?" Derrick was looking at him but Doreen stood to begin clearing the dishes.

Benito mentally shook himself. "Sorry! I wasn't listening! I was organizing my plan of attack on these jobs that Aunt Doreen has given me." He grinned and Derrick returned his smile.

"I was just suggesting to your Aunt here, that as you worked so hard today, you could have a break tomorrow and we could all go in to the Stampede, what do you think?" Benito blinked. He had no idea what the 'Stampede' was.

Doreen saved him. "Of course he would like to!"

"Yes," Benito joined in her enthusiasm, "That sounds terrific!" He assumed it would be. Whatever it was!

After helping Doreen clear up the meal, Benito and she went into the basement and began sorting some boxes and putting the ones she did not want straight away, onto the shelves, letting Benito reach the higher ones. Although Doreen was tall for a woman, Benito was still a couple of inches taller.

"Really," she said, "I don't know why we brought so much stuff from our last house." She pointed to a couple of boxes beside her. "These can all go to the charity shop. They are books that we have read and will not read again. We can NOT keep everything!"

"And these," she pointed to three others, "are clothes that your uncle will never fit into again! I don't care what he says, he will never again fit into a 34-inch waist." She lower her voice, and added in a mischievous whisper, "Just don't tell your Uncle Derrick that we have given them away!"

Benito smiled down at her as she sat on the small stool in the storage room.

"I mean," she carried on, obviously on a roll, "a storage area is to store things that you will use again, not to store things that you will never take off the shelf until you move the next time!"

Benito nodded, "You are quite right, Aunt Doreen." He and his mother did not have stuff they did not use. In fact, they had very little. Sometimes it bothered him, when he heard other kids talk about their laptops and PS4 games and iPhones. He and his mother shared an old desktop computer, and the phone he had was a basic smartphone that his uncle Tadeo had given him so he could keep an eye on Benito when he was 'working' for him. Funny to call it that – working – since the only payment he received was to not get hit if he obeyed.

"What do you think?"

Doreen's voice entered his thoughts and he shook himself slightly and turned to her. "Sorry, I was not paying attention," he apologized. "I'm afraid my mind wandered off for a minute!"

"I see that! What were you thinking of so deeply?" she queried. "You had quite a distressed look on your face," she added, concerned.

Benito's face flushed slightly as he scrambled for a reply. "Uh … I … uh … was thinking of a friend of mine, back in England." He paused, trying desperately to think of what to say. "And he is quite poor … uh … so he doesn't have a lot of stuff … and his … uh … Dad hits him." He looked into Doreen's sympathetic eyes, hoping she would not question his stuttering reply.

She looked at him sadly, fortunately misunderstanding his hesitant response. "Sometimes these things are hard to talk about." She tilted her head slightly as she continued gently, "Does anyone know his dad hurts him?"

Benito could feel pain stabbing the back of his eyes as panic filtered into his veins. He was not good at making up stories and wished he had just said he was thinking of something private that he did not want to talk about. He swallowed and breathed deeply, straining for a sensible story to relate to Doreen.

"Um … his mom knows … um … in fact, she has left his dad now and … is living in a refuge for battered women and their children." He began to gain momentum. "They left just before I came over and will be staying there for a few weeks … till they get his mom's passport renewed … so they can leave England and move to New York to live with her parents." He paused, wondering if the story sounded plausible.

Doreen looked slightly doubtful, thought for a moment, then smiled comfortingly at him. "That is good that they have a place to go, but it is sad for you to have your friend leave." Benito just pursed his lips, bending his head slightly, as if in deep thought about his 'friend'. He dare not say anything else.

Doreen stood up, stretching her legs. "Well, we have done some good work here tonight, I think after your hard day in the garden you ought to hit the hay at a reasonable time. You want to have a good rest before we head off to the Stampede tomorrow, and we want to leave at 9:30, to get a good day in."

Benito nodded enthusiastically, still completely ignorant about what he was agreeing to, but confident that if it was something Toby would enjoy, he would too. He kissed Doreen on the cheek and said goodnight, leaving her in the store room to pick up a few bits before she headed upstairs.

Benito looked in the reflection of the bathroom mirror as he brushed his teeth, examining his features. What were the chances of him finding someone who looked so much like him? They could be brothers. Perhaps they could be friends. No, stupid thought. He had just arranged for Toby's unpleasant and most likely, painful trip. Toby would probably pummel Benito himself if got the chance. Benito rinsed and spit, putting his toothbrush in the holder by the sink. No, it would probably be best if he never met Toby again.

⇒●⇐

WEDNESDAY 4th July – Nicaragua

Pain brought him to consciousness and Toby groaned in agony as the harsh morning light shone through the glassless window frame. He was still bound and he struggled to get comfortable on his lumpy mattress. If only they would untie him. Or at least loosen the knots a bit. He could really do with a stretch. He glanced over at Gwen as he suddenly realized she was watching him.

"So who are you, and what do you have to do with everything?" she looked at him accusingly, as though he was responsible for her predicament.

"I have no idea," he responded helplessly.

"What, you have no idea who you are?" she said suspiciously.

"No, I know who I am, but I have no idea why I am here or how I got on the plane to Nicaragua. It was supposed to be Benito."

"So who is this Benito guy, anyway? They sure seem desperate to find him." She looked at him expectantly, waiting for answers, but Toby had none to give.

Just then, Rebeca came cheerfully through the door, with two plates of something that Toby assumed was to be their breakfast. He was ravenous and could have eaten almost anything. He remembered yesterday's breakfast and thought about Emmie. He smiled up at Rebeca as she placed the dish beside him, and she smiled warmly back. On the plate was something that looked like beans and rice, sliced avocado, and tortilla.

"Thank you," Toby said gratefully. Then paused as he wondered how he was going to eat it with his hands bound. He gathered she would not be allowed to loosen the ties. She gave Gwen her food and turned back to Toby.

"I realize it is a bit degrading, but it would probably be best if I fed you. Is that all right?"

He wondered at her placing importance on his dignity, but nodded. "Thanks, that will be fine."

Rebeca helped him sit in some fashion, and then waited a moment with the bowl in her hand.

"You can give me some now," he said, wondering what she was waiting for.

"I thought you might want to say grace first." Toby looked at her with raised eyebrows.

"Don't you think it is kind of odd that your people have drugged me and bound me and now you want to say grace?" Toby was annoyed, but Rebeca responded without hesitation.

"It was not my people. It was Tadeo and his men. Tadeo and my father were childhood friends. Tadeo's father was British and when he and his sister were young teenagers, he took them and their mother to England. Unfortunately, Tadeo quickly made friends with criminals. He is always up to no good, but the police have never caught him. My father lets him come back and stay here. Sometimes he comes to just wait in between 'jobs', but sometimes he brings his trouble with him." She nodded towards Gwen, and Gwen frowned at her. "Tadeo has been doing more and more wicked things. My father has finally told him that this time, when he is finished his business, he must leave and never come back. He felt a loyalty to Tadeo, because when they were little, Tadeo saved my father from drowning in a river. But my father said he can no longer turn a blind eye to Tadeo's wrongdoings."

"What…"

"Hey!" Gwen interrupted, as she finished a mouthful. "I haven't had a wash since I got here. I stink. I should be allowed to have a bath or a shower. And what about some clean clothes? They didn't let me pack any of mine, but I could fit into yours." She looked over at Rebeca's full figure and back at her slender one. " Well, they would probably be way too big, and probably not very attractive, but they would be better than nothing." Toby raised his eyebrows at her rudeness, but Rebeca smiled over her shoulder good-naturedly.

"I will see if they will let me take you to the river. You can wash there. I do have a simple dress that will fit you, and some underthings. You can wear them while I wash yours."

"The river?! That will be cold! Can't you heat me up some water? I cannot wash in a river! What if someone sees me?" She paused for another mouthful of food. "And can't you find me anything decent for breakfast? This is something that should be served for lunch, and not every day! I am used to muesli and yoghurt with some freshly squeezed orange juice. Surely you have some oranges you can squeeze for me?" She looked over at Rebeca with furrowed eyebrows, but as her gaze passed over Toby, her eyes softened and she half smiled.

"Loquacious, isn't she?" Rebeca said softly to Toby. He raised one eyebrow.

"Loquacious?" he queried.

"Someone who chatters a lot." She added, "I go to a school in a town a few miles away, Tudela. There is a kind teacher there who is English. She gave me a dictionary for my birthday, and I decided to try to regularly learn new words. I found that one yesterday." She paused for a moment before continuing. "My mother was British and she taught me to speak English. Father felt that I only needed to know Spanish, and that English was unnecessary, but he let her teach me anyway."

Toby caught the past tense and asked cautiously, "What happened to your mom?"

Rebeca's eyes saddened. "She got a fever. Father would not take her to the hospital. Our people are wary of white medicine. But our sukia, our medicine man, could not help her with his medicines. I do not know what it was. We never found out. She died two weeks after she first got ill. That was five years ago, when I was thirteen."

She stood up as she put the last spoonful into Toby's mouth. "You had better prepare yourself, Toby. The men will be back soon, and they will want some answers." She took his and Gwen's bowl and went out the door.

Toby bit his lip thoughtfully. Why did Benito not just bring his uncle the diamonds? Toby thought back to his introduction to Tadeo. He supposed Benito was afraid, but surely his uncle would not have hurt his own flesh and blood. What had happened to Benito? Had Benito taken his flight to Canada? Toby's aunt and uncle must be worried sick about him when he did not arrive. They and his parents would have the authorities looking for him. But then, how would they know where to look? If Benito used his ticket, as far as the airline was concerned, Toby Myers had boarded the plane in London and landed in Calgary, then probably disappeared, completely. And if Benito had stayed in England? What then? Toby doubted that Benito would admit to anyone what he had done. There was no point in sitting and waiting to be rescued. No one was coming.

CHAPTER 6

Toby heard the men laughing and shouting as they returned. They sounded drunk. His heart started racing at the thought of being interrogated by Tadeo and his buddies. He had no idea where Benito was, but would they believe him? Somehow, Toby did not think so.

A moment later, Tadeo and two other men similar in colouring to himself but with black eyes, burst through the feeble wooden door, nearly breaking it from its hinges. Gwen curled up fearfully into a tight ball like a frightened kitten on a corner of her mat and watched anxiously as the men walked over to Toby and yanked him to a sitting position.

"Ow!" Toby called out in agony as all his injuries started hurting at once. "That hurts." He wasn't sure why he said that. He doubted they would care.

Tadeo's eyes glared in anger as he put his dark greasy face close to Toby's, their noses nearly touching. His hot breath was rancid with stale alcohol and Toby nearly gagged.

"Where is he?!" Tadeo shouted at Toby in a rage. "Where is Benito, the little swine?!" Toby impulsively leaned back and fell against the wooden wall, banging his head hard. He winced from the added pain and unbidden tears welled up. He blinked them away quickly. As scared as he was, Toby did not want this man to know he was afraid. His pride wouldn't let him.

Tadeo grabbed Toby by the throat and pulled him back towards him. The other two men stood watching with sinister grins. Toby gasped for breath as Tadeo squeezed his big hands around his throat, shouting again, "Where is Benito?!"

The men behind him started laughing, and one said, "He can't speak if you don't stop squeezing his neck!" Tadeo shook his hands to the side and tried to compose himself as

Toby coughed and choked, wheezing in air through his painful throat.

"I … I don't know," he sputtered. "I have no idea where he is."

"Of course you do, you stupid boy! You must know where you were going when that stupid nephew of mine did the switch on you. He texted me to say there had been problems and he was swapping places with a boy that looked like him. He said he was going to spend the summer helping a couple move into their new home!"

Toby's heart sank. Benito was impersonating him? Surely Aunt Doreen and Uncle Derrick would know straight away. Or would they? It had been five years since he had seen them. He supposed enough time had gone by for them to be fooled. Benito really had looked an awful lot like him.

"Well?!" Tadeo was in his face again, and he spat as he shouted in a rage. "Surely you know where your aunt and uncle live? How about a telephone number?!"

Toby hesitated. Would Tadeo hurt his uncle and aunt? Maybe he would just get a hold of his nephew and … what? Toby did not know what to do.

SMACK! Toby fell sideways at the force of Tadeo's fist on the side of his head, and he cried out in agony as the pain pulsated through his head. The ringing in his ear was deafening, and the spinning room disorientated him. With bound hands and feet, he could neither escape or defend himself.

"Ummpfff!" Toby was thrown against the wall and he heard a crack in his chest as he bounced off the wall and landed on a small but sturdy table. The stabbing pain in his chest was muffled by the excruciating agony in his head. He was beyond tears and he begged God to make Tadeo stop. Toby could hear the men's laughter in the distance as he felt himself drifting away.

He half opened his eyes into the nightmare and saw Tadeo coming for him again. He tried to lift his bound hands to shield himself as Tadeo took another swing, but he was too slow and he heard another loud smack as Tadeo's fist made contact with his face. Toby vaguely heard a girl screaming, then gratefully welcomed the blackness.

———◆———

WEDNESDAY 4th July – Canada

Benito opened his eyes and smiled at the sunshine streaming through the window that was just above the grass outside. He folded his arms behind his head and relaxed in the pleasant warmth of the new day, wondering what this 'Stampede' was. Derrick and Doreen seemed to think he would really enjoy himself there, so he assumed it was something that a sixteen, or in his case, seventeen year old boy would like. He sighed contentedly. He could not remember feeling so happy.

Throwing back the covers, Benito swung his feet out of bed and crouched down in front of Toby's bag, digging through it to find something cool. Evidently this Stampede was an outside thing, that much, he had managed to learn. He found a blue and green plaid short sleeved shirt and some light khaki shorts, then dug a little deeper and found some fresh boxers. He changed quickly, feeling quite pleased that everything fit so perfectly. *Everything* was perfect.

"Toby!" he heard Aunt Doreen call down to him. He almost thought of the couple as his real aunt and uncle, now. They had made him feel like family. He laughed. Well, he supposed he WAS family in their eyes!

"Coming!" he called up. He quickly pulled the covers up in a haphazard manner and trotted out the door and up the stairs. An appetizing smell of bacon and eggs greeted him at the top step. He might actually gain weight this summer!

An hour later, the three of them were in Doreen's little hatchback and heading north in the baking sunshine. After a short drive, they were in the big city and soon parked in a crowded car park. Benito could see why they did not want to bring Derrick's mustang. The attendants had the cars packed in tightly so they could make as much money as possible. He looked in amazement at the streams of people heading in one direction. Many of them wore cowboy hats and boots and Benito chuckled. He did not realize people actually wore those these days! Everyone looked elated and chattered away excitedly.

Doreen gave Derrick his crutches and locked up the car. Benito looked at Derrick, concerned.

"How far do we have to walk?" Asked Benito.

Doreen smiled at his concern. "Don't worry, we just go down the road a bit and across the street. The entrance is not far away, and they have wheel chairs to rent right at the gate. Benito nodded and they let Derrick set the pace as they followed the crowds.

A few moments later, they had joined a throng in front of a large entrance. Above him was a huge red 'C' sat on top of sideways 'S', and underneath was written 'Calgary Stampede' Beyond the entrance, he could see a fairground with various rides reaching into the sky. Smells of burgers and cotton candy drifted out and despite his large breakfast, Benito's stomach growled. This was going to be another great day!

Immediately inside the park, there was a place to rent wheelchairs. Doreen handed over some money, then chose one for Derrick and wheeled it over. He just stood leaning on his crutches and frowned down at it.

"Derrick," she said determinedly, "You can NOT go all around the park on crutches for the whole day!" He sighed and submitting reluctantly, sat down, handing her his crutches. She looked at them for a moment, then walked back over to the man she had just paid. He took them from her and promised to keep them safe until the end of the day.

They wandered around for a little while, looking at all the various attractions, then Doreen stopped at a roller-coaster called the Outlaw and surprised Benito by taking him by the arm and joining the queue. Each car fit four people, and a young couple joined Benito and Doreen in their bright pink and green car. They both screamed with delight, as did the couple behind them, as they raced around the track and Benito gasped when they crawled up to the highest point and he saw the grounds, the city and out in the west, the blue Rocky Mountains with just a slight topping of snow. The view lasted only seconds as the car appeared to go over the edge, and then plummet down the track and around a corner then back up and down and around until Benito became delightfully disorientated.

Derrick watched contentedly from the confines of his chair. He hated rides. Doreen and Benito were both dizzy and excited as they filed out of the gate when the ride ended, talking animatedly about which ride to go on next. They decided on the Crazy Mouse roller-coaster which was made up mainly of hairpin turns, and they raced back and forth, appearing to be heading off the track each time the car took another sharp turn.

They then took a slightly tamer ride, the Wave Swinger, which was made up of many swings that took them high in the sky as they swung around in a large circle over and over, until Benito's head was spinning.

When they got off, he could barely stand up straight, so Doreen decided the three of them should go on the Giant

Wheel. The wait was longer in the line-up to that ride, as it was suitable for people of all ages and ranges of bravery. It was definitely a more sedate ride, but Benito enjoyed it nonetheless, being able to take in the view again at a more leisurely pace as it reached up to 50 metres high.

Twenty minutes later, Derrick was back in his wheelchair, watching Doreen and Benito swinging in their orange car as they rode up the Zipper. Benito barely got his land legs back before Doreen had him lining up to get on Spinout, a 45-foot rotating claw that spun in all directions, including upside down.

Benito was feeling quite nauseous after that, and neither he nor Doreen could walk properly for several minutes.

"I think we should try out some games for a bit, so your Uncle Derrick does not feel left out, hey?" Doreen suggested.

Benito was silently pleased to rest his stomach and head, and give his legs time to regain strength. He felt like he had been at sea for weeks. He looked at Doreen and thought she looked a little pale. Perhaps she was not as tough as he thought she was!

The first game they came to was a shooting game. To win a prize, you had to shoot three deer as they 'ran' across a field. Benito thought the metal deer looked rather small and moved rather fast, so he decided to just let Derrick have a go. Derrick handed over some tickets and grasped the plastic rifle in front of him. He had ten tries to get the three deer, and he managed to get his three in only seven tries, and was annoyed with the man running the game when he told him that it was against the rules to use his last three tries to hit another three deer. Even though the selection of cuddly toys that he was offered were rather small and ugly, he still felt ripped off! Benito was rather impressed with Derrick for arguing with the well built, bald man who had a skull and cross bones tattooed on both arms. Doreen stepped in before there was any trouble and just grabbed a soft blue cheap looking teddy bear from the choice that the man offered before she pushed Derrick away.

"I don't know why you have to do that, honey," she complained to Derrick while he was still moaning about getting 'robbed'. "If those are the rules, those are the rules. Besides," she giggled, "did you REALLY want TWO of those ugly cuddly toys?!"

"Well," said Derrick, still scowling, but seeing the funny side, "I've never shot so well! I think I might go in a wheelchair next year on these games!"

They all tried their hand at the next game: throwing balls at stuffed beavers as they popped up from a wooden dam. Again, Derrick did very well. Benito surprised himself at his own accuracy.

Following that, they each grabbed a water pistol and tried to shoot ducks off a pond. Doreen became very enthusiastic when she got more ducks than Derrick, and she squealed with delight as she jumped up in triumph. Unfortunately, she lost her balance and, with her hand still firmly on the trigger, accidentally aimed the cold water at the young red headed woman managing the game, squirting her squarely in the face. The three stood silent for a moment, and Doreen covered her mouth in embarrassment, but the girl just smiled, and the three burst into raucous laughter. Nevertheless, they decided unanimously that it would be a good idea to move on to a different game.

After a while, and not a few cuddly toys later, Doreen decided she wanted one more ride before lunch. Against his better judgment, Benito agreed to go on the ride with her. Six people sat in each car, that twisted around and around, as the whole ride itself, went around in a circle and up and down.

Doreen threw her head back and roared with laughter as they both stepped off the ride and wobbled over to where they had left Derrick in the welcome shade of a tree. He just raised one eyebrow and shook his head. Doreen barely managed to push Derrick over to a picnic bench in the shade, and she had to sit down for a moment to orientate herself.

A few minutes later, she was recovered and left Derrick by the bench as she and Benito went to three different food outlets to get what each of them wanted. Finally, they sat down exhausted and thirsty. Each took a long sip from their drink before tucking in. They were all so hungry, that for several minutes, no one said anything as they each just sat contentedly enjoying their food.

Benito spoke first. "You don't know what you are missing, Uncle Derrick, not going on rides – they are so much fun!"

Derrick grunted. "About as much fun as rolling down a hill in a barrel." He picked up a paper serviette and wiped some grease off of his chin, then continued to eat his huge bacon and egg hamburger.

Doreen poked at her pasta salad and paused as she lifted her fork to her mouth, "Darling, it is not at all the same thing. You cannot get hurt on a ride."

Derrick raised an eyebrow. "I didn't say they were the same, I just said I would enjoy them the same."

"Well, how would you know?" she continued stubbornly, "You've never been in a barrel rolling down a hill."

"And I have never been on an amusement ride, but I am very observant and I have an adequate imagination to decide what each would be like," he answered dryly, with only the twinkle in his eyes belying the humour.

"Oh Derrick, why are you so analytical?"

He laughed, "Why can't you just accept that some people don't like rides? We can't all be like you, sweetheart!" He looked at Benito with a look of mock horror on his face. "Can you imagine what the world would be like if everyone was like your aunt??!"

Benito laughed and Doreen punched Derrick's shoulder playfully.

"Ow! Husband abuse!" Derrick nodded at Benito, "You'll be my witness, won't you, son?"

Benito smiled as he popped his last fry in his mouth and slurped the last of his coke through the straw. He sighed deeply with pleasure, and just sat looking at everything and everyone around him. It had been a terrific morning, even with the intense heat.

Doreen looked at her watch: it was 1:40. "I have tickets for the rodeo at 2:00, we had better get a move on!"

She and Benito gathered all their rubbish and tossed it in the bin, then Doreen grabbed the handles of the wheel chair and pulled Derrick away from the end of the bench, leaning him back at a precarious angle before charging ahead at a quick pace.

"Doreen!" he cried out in a panic, and she answered with a giggle.

"I've got you!" then she turned with a jerk, pushed him forward even more exuberantly and headed off to the rodeo grounds at a quick march. Benito increased the length of his stride to catch up, amazed at her energy.

They reached the rodeo grounds and a helpful young man pointed them to the wheelchair access. They had very good seats with a space at the side for Derrick's wheelchair. With ten minutes to spare, Doreen dashed off to get three more drinks, and arrived back just as the first event began.

Benito marvelled at the bravery of the men who attempted to ride huge, angry bulls that jumped and raged around the ring as they tried to unmount the cowboys on top of them.

And he marvelled even more at the valiant, crazily dressed clowns as they danced around the arena, waving their arms and brightly coloured handkerchiefs to draw the snorting bull's attention away from men who had fallen off the crazed beasts. How courageous they were as they risked their lives for others! He envied them. Man after man took up the challenge and a great cheer roared through the crowd when a man finally lasted until the buzzer.

Then came the steer wrestling. Benito watched with rapt attention as men on horseback raced after steers, swung their lassos that went sailing through the air towards the steer and, if they were good, hooked on their horns and stopped the steers in their tracks. Then they would jump off their horses and grabbing the horns, wrestled the large animals to the ground with lightning speed. How strong they must be!

He was amazed at the adventurous spirits of the women, as well. His eyes were glued on the women as they rode beautiful horses that galloped along with amazing speed around three barrels, desperate to beat the time of the previous contestant. The thought of getting on a horse standing still, terrified Benito; but to have the courage and ability to stay on an animal tearing down the arena and leaning at 45 degrees as they rounded each barrel, was something beyond Benito's comprehension.

Benito was so enthralled with the rodeo that he did not notice as the time ticked by, and when it was over and Doreen announced it was 5:00, he was shocked.

"How about another ride on the roller-coaster, Toby?" Doreen asked, and Derrick groaned. She turned her attention to her husband. "I don't want to leave just yet, because we will hit traffic." Looking back at Benito, she said, "Are you game?"

Benito was actually tired, but he was not about to admit he had less energy than this woman, so he nodded his head with pretended eagerness and they headed back towards the Crazy Mouse.

In fact, Doreen dragged him on another couple of rides, but by the end of the day Benito was pleasurably exhausted. He pushed Derrick back to the entrance and they picked up his crutches. They all made their way wearily back to the car in the warm July evening.

Five minutes after they got in the car and headed out of the city, Benito fell asleep. He awoke just as they were rolling up the steep drive to the blue house that Benito was beginning to think of as home. What a wonderful life. Benito could not bring himself to think of the summer ending and going back to England. Maybe there was some way he could stay here forever. There must be something he could do to avoid ever seeing his uncle again.

Doreen entered the house first, and hung the keys on the rack, while Benito helped Derrick up the few steps from the garage into a large, comfortable armchair in the living room. Benito sat in a chair beside him, silent for a moment, and lost in the day's memories.

Toby's mom's voice interrupted his thoughts, "Aunt Dor, we got an amazing last minute deal on a two week holiday to Mauritius with the girls, and we head off tomorrow. I'll call you when we get back!"

Doreen was listening to the answering machine. Benito decided to get a drink of water and headed into the kitchen where she stood. He stopped dead in his tracks at the next voice.

"Benito! You little *******! You better get your **** down here! I want the rest of my package! You've got three days to get down here or your friend is going to suffer even more of my wrath than he already has, you swine!" A loud bang rang through the kitchen as he slammed the phone down, and Doreen covered her mouth in shock at the coarse language. Benito stood with his mouth open as Derrick turned, a grave, puzzled concern in his eyes. Benito's glorious summer had been cut drastically short.

CHAPTER 7

Had Benito been able to close his mouth and bring the colour back to his face that had disappeared at the sound of his uncle's voice, he might have been able to pretend ignorance. However, the evil that seethed out of the answering machine transcended the distance between them, defeating him completely and he collapsed in a nearby chair, covering his face and weeping profusely.

"I'm sorry! I'm sorry!" he cried out, over and over, rocking back and forth in his distress.

"What is the matter, Toby? Do you know this Benito? Who is he?" Benito sobbed louder as even now, this trusting couple were still believing him. What had he done? Even worse, what had Uncle Tadeo done to Toby? Suddenly, he was overcome with extreme guilt in the face of his being discovered.

It was several minutes before Benito managed to stop his sobbing, but with Doreen and Derrick on either side, each with a loving arm around him, he blubbered incomprehensibly, trying to explain what had happened. He took a breath and looked into their blank faces. He looked from one to the other helplessly.

"I'm not Toby! He is in Nicaragua," he finally gasped. The hurt shock on their faces set Benito off again, and the couple could do nothing but embrace him as he wept into their arms.

Finally, Benito emptied himself of his self pity and guilt, and his sobbing subsided. He sat slumped, with his head hung down to his chest.

Desperate to find out more about what happened to Toby and where he could be, but not wanting to trigger another outburst, the couple sat in silence beside him, waiting. And praying.

After several long minutes, Benito took a mammoth gulp of air, then began at the first holiday he spent with his uncle and, speaking quickly so he would not start blubbering again, finished when he waved goodbye to Toby at Heathrow, and then watched him head onto the wrong plane, to Nicaragua.

Now it was Derrick and Doreen's turn to be speechless. It was a truly unbelievable story, and yet, they both immediately sensed it to be true. Feelings of immense dread for their nephew argued with their overwhelming compassion for this pitiable boy that they still held between them.

"Well," said Doreen eventually, looking at Benito seriously. He could barely manage to return her gaze. "It looks like you and I are going to have to take a trip to Nicaragua." Derrick's eyes widened.

"What?! It has been a long time since we were there, we were young then!"

Benito turned to Doreen questioningly. She replied, "We went on a missionary trip to Central America when we were fresh out of college – that's how we met." She turned to her husband lovingly, despite the horror that had just unfolded.

"What else is there to do, honey? Emily and David are unreachable, and it could take some explaining, if they believe us at all, to get someone in authority to do something, and quickly. I am not sure how *I* can believe it." She glanced down at his cast. "And *you* certainly cannot go down there." They held each other's gaze for a moment. "There's no other option!"

As their voices grew agitated, Benito began to sniffle. Derrick patted his knee tenderly.

"What you did was ... well ... you know what it was. But we understand how frightened you must have been to do this." He paused for a long moment, forcing out his next few words. "And we forgive you Tob ... Benito." Doreen nodded. Benito could not believe his ears.

"You forgive me?!" he turned from one to the other. "But why?!"

"Grace, son." He took a deep breath, "Grace."

Benito looked at him blankly.

"Grace is giving something that someone does not deserve. God gave His Son Jesus to die for our sins – that is the ultimate gift of grace." Benito still looked slightly bemused, but Derrick, despite saying the words, did not actually feel the grace in his heart and could not manage a clearer explanation at that moment.

Doreen can tell you about it on the trip down. There will be plenty of time." He paused for a moment, thinking. "Joe!" he burst out. "I am going to call Joe. He's on summer break from university. He can meet you in Managua."

"But," Doreen started to protest, but saw the determination in her husband's eyes and knew not to argue. Besides, it was probably a good idea.

So while Doreen searched for flights to Nicaragua, Derrick called Joe, Toby's older brother in England, and explained the situation with as little detail as possible, which was quite difficult as Joe fired questions at him in disbelieving panic. Finally, he just said Doreen would explain when they met up, but not to worry. Derrick nearly choked on his words. The worry was welling up in him like a volcano ready to explode.

Fortunately, Derrick and Doreen had a reasonable amount in their savings account. Doreen arranged Joe's flight as close to theirs as possible, and in the end, he would only have a two-hour wait for them if both flights were on time. The best she could do was two days from now; it didn't give them much time when they arrived. Doreen prayed it would be enough.

THURSDAY 5th July – Nicaragua

Toby's little legs pedalled his new red mountain bike as fast as they could, but his brother was pulling away in the distance on his old blue racer. He started to panic and pedalled faster. He was not sure of the way home; what if he got lost? The path was particularly stony at that point and hard to negotiate. The wheels bounced as much as they rolled along the ground, but fear kept Toby struggling on as he watched Joe's angry figure growing smaller. As he fixed his eyes on his brother, Toby lost sight of the steep, rocky quarry to the left of the path. Neither did he see the edge creep closer; and closer. Alarm filled his young body at the thought of being alone in the woods, spurring him on; his pudgy hands growing clammy as he grasped the foam handle bars tightly. He vaguely noticed a bright red sign flash past, but was too young to read the word DANGER. A burst of adrenaline raced down to his feet and he pushed down hard, too hard, slipping off the pedal, gouging his ankle. Toby jerked to the left in pain, tipping the bike sharply. He screamed as empty space rose up at him and large sharp rocks beckoned wickedly along the steep slope and floor.

Toby opened his eyes, squinting at the bright light that glared down at him from the warm blue summer afternoon sky. It felt like his entire body had been alternately beaten with a hammer, and stabbed with a knife. Never, in his few years of life, had he known such debilitating agony. His left leg twitched and he cried out in torment. Even the very breaths he took were severely laboured as his ribs complained viciously at the movement. He gasped out his brother's name in a whisper and closed his eyes at the effort. "Joe!"

"Toby!" he faintly heard his brother calling from some distant place. Was his brother crying? He never saw his brother cry before. He was five years older than Toby. Ten year old boys don't cry, do they? Toby felt pebbles cascading down on him and flinched as each one struck him unforgivingly. A hand touched his face and he looked up at Joe's terrified blurred eyes.

"Hey, Joe," he breathed out weakly, "You didn't leave me, after all." He heard Joe crying. Then silence consumed him.

Bright lights brought Toby back to consciousness. But this time, it wasn't the sun. He was in a white room with huge ceiling lights and people all around him. Frightened, Toby tried to sit up, but was pushed back down gently by warm strong hands.

"You had quite a nasty fall, sweetheart," an unfamiliar, but calming voice said. He started to relax then realized he had something covering his mouth. Panicking, he tried to pull it off but found the movement restrained by a tube sticking out of his arm.

"It is OK, Toby, you are in the hospital, just relax and lie back down. The mask will help you to breath easier and the tube is making your pain better." The soothing voice and the realization that his pain had lessened, quietened his heart rate and he drifted back to sleep.

"Toby, darling, Mommy and Daddy are here," tender lips kissed his cheek and Toby was once again brought back to consciousness and opened his eyes as soft, loving fingers stroked his forehead. The severe lights had given way to softer ones; he was in a different room. The thing over his face was gone, but he found he was still attached to the tube.

"Mommy!" he cried as she leaned over and embraced him tightly. "Ow!" he called out.

"Sorry, Tobs," she smiled down at him. "I am just so glad you are OK!" Joe and his dad stood on the other side of the bed.

"I ... I'm sorry I threw ... that chunk of mud at you, Joe," he finally managed. "I ... didn't know ... there was a rock in it." Joe reached over and tousled his hair gently.

"Don't sweat it, buddy," he smiled, the good news that the doctor had just given them washing over him. "We're cool."

"I brought Flopsy Bunny for you to cuddle," said his mom as she handed him his cuddly toy, worn ragged from love. Toby reached out and held Flopsy tight to his sore chest. As he held her she seemed to grow warmer. And firmer. He looked at her curiously. Was she breathing?

"Toby, I have a drink for you, do you think you can manage it?" Toby turned at the strange voice and looked up into the familiar faces. No one else seemed to have heard the girl's voice. "Toby?" He looked down at Flopsy and she smiled up at him. Toby jerked in surprise, and was instantly transported back to the hut.

Emmie sat curled up in a tight ball by his chest purring quietly. His arms wrapped tightly around her and he wondered that she didn't try to escape from his fierce grip. He suddenly realized he was only looking at her with one eye and, panicking, his hand went to his left eye where he felt a large swelling. Beside his bed, Rebeca crouched with a drink in one hand. With the other, she gently took his hand off his eye and spoke comfortingly to him.

"It's OK, just a bit of swelling. It will go down in a day or two." She nodded towards Emmie.

"This little one was hanging around the outskirts of our village all day yesterday. After your beating, she became brave and ventured in. She is your friend?"

"Yes, she gave me my first breakfast here." He looked down at her affectionately, giving her soft head a little scratch.

Rebeca looked back at Toby, and her face became sober. "I removed your restraints, and got our sukia to give you something for the pain and you slept through the rest of yesterday. My father is very angry with Tadeo for doing this to you." She scowled and Toby's lips curled slightly at the thought that Rebeca could probably be quite fierce if need be. She looked at him puzzled, her arm stretched out to give him the coconut milk.

"What are you smiling at? You should be thoroughly miserable, considering Tadeo's beating. Your one eye is nearly swollen shut." She paused. "I am sorry I woke you but you were distressed as you slept. Were you dreaming about Tadeo?" She put a hand behind his head to help him towards the drink. His body welcomed the cool liquid that ran down the back of his throat.

Toby paused, then answered the latter question. "No, actually, I was dreaming about an accident I had when I was a little boy. I fell into a quarry and bruised every part of my body, but luckily nothing was broken."

"There is no such thing as luck," Rebeca interrupted him. "God's authority prevails in all things. *He* decided that you would have no bones broken."

"Uh … yah …" He paused, not knowing how to answer. "Anyway, the doctor said little children seem to know how to fall! They go limp, whereas adults stiffen up. I suppose stunt men train themselves to fall like little children, that's how they can fall and not injure themselves. Like when they fall down stairs and things."

"Stunt men?" Rebeca queried. Toby looked around him at the sparseness.

"Have you ever seen a movie?" he asked. She shook her head.

"No, I have heard of them, though. The teachers at our school sometimes tell us about such things."

Toby's glance caught his back pack, pulled open with the contents strewn carelessly beside him. Rebeca followed his gaze.

"Tadeo was looking for your aunt and uncle's information. He must have found it, because he shouted with much delight and waved a piece of paper in the air before hurrying out." Fear gripped Toby. His mom had insisted on writing Doreen and Derrick's phone number and address on a piece of paper and put it in his back pack in case Toby lost his phone.

"What will he do?" he asked her, worriedly.

"He wants the rest of the diamonds so he can give me back to my parents," piped up Gwen, who up until now had just been watching and listening silently.

Rebeca continued, "I heard him tell his men he was going into Rama, a large town a couple of miles north of Tudela. It has a telephone line. He is going to make a phone call to his nephew and give him three days to bring the rest of the diamonds down here."

"But I ..." Toby broke off, and looked down at Emmie who seemed to be grinning widely at him. He stroked her head, surprised at how calming the act was. Something told him to keep quiet about the rest of the diamonds. It was probably best that no one knew he had them. He looked up at Rebeca; she looked worried.

Rebeca gazed over her shoulder at Gwen then looked back at Toby, whispering, "My father and the men have gone hunting. I am worried about what Tadeo will do to you both when he gets back. I overheard him telling those other men that he does not plan on taking Gwen back. He ... he said he was just going to ... dispose of you and her in the jungle. He said he did not want any witnesses..." her voice trailed off and Gwen called out.

"Hey, what are you talking to Toby about? Didn't your parents ever teach you that whispering was rude?"

Rebeca continued to whisper, "My father may not be back until tomorrow. He told Tadeo to be gone when he got back. He had no idea Tadeo had become so wicked. He is not a bad man, my father. He just felt obligated to let Tadeo stay here. He had no idea of the full plan, and my father naively believed that Tadeo respected him enough to leave you and Gwen alone, and just go."

Toby looked at Rebeca thoughtfully, the gravity of their circumstances slowly sinking into his murky brain. "We need to go," he said suddenly, loud enough for Gwen to hear. Rebeca nodded her head in agreement.

"Go?!" cried Gwen, "Where?! That man is going to take me to the British Embassy in Managua."

Rebeca cleared her throat and spoke gently, "There is no British Embassy in Managua, Gwen. He was lying to you." She paused, trying to be kind, but there was no kindness to be found in the grisly truth. "He has ... other plans for you." Gwen turned pale and curled herself up tightly.

"How are we going to escape?" asked Toby, trying to think clearly.

Rebeca turned back to him and smiled mischievously. "I have already begun a plan. My father has made some fermented cassava. Tadeo's men have a weakness for that. They were pleased to partake in some generous servings on this very hot day! This is our rainy season, and we usually get a heavy rain for an hour or a half each day, but it has been unusually dry for a couple of days. This will help us."

She stood to leave, then added, "It should not be too much longer." She shook her head reproachfully, "They drink quickly." And she hurried out the door. Toby chuckled to himself that Rebeca should pause to disapprove of something when it was clearly going to work to their advantage.

Toby struggled to sit up and Emmie bounced off, landing on the window frame. "Ugghh!" he said as the movement awakened the pain of the earlier beating. He looked down at his chest that had been neatly wrapped. Rebeca was quite the nurse. Well, he assumed it must be her that was cleaning and bandaging his myriad of wounds.

"We should get organized so we are ready to go the moment Rebeca says it is time." Toby looked over at Gwen's terrified face.

"Do we really have to go?! Now?!" Her bottom lip quivered and she curled up even tighter. "Can't we just wait for that man? Surely he will do as he promised."

Toby did not know what to say, so he just shook his head grimly. Fear welled up in her eyes as Gwen reluctantly grasped their fate.

Toby began stuffing his belongings back in the pack, grimacing at his complaining injuries. He paused a moment as he picked up the Nintendo DS that hid the diamonds, looking at the seemingly innocuous game thoughtfully. He might need them to bargain for his safety. He bit his lip pensively. Had that been Benito's intention when he hid them? Had Benito kept them back to guarantee his own safety from his uncle?

His movements slowed as he picked up his shirt and tried to put it on. Gwen saw his struggle and moved to his side to help him. He was pleasantly surprised at her sudden burst of compassion, but became embarrassed as he leaned on her to stand and realized he was just in his boxers. Seemingly unfazed, she picked his shorts off the ground and helped him step into them. They had just finished tying up Toby's trainers as Rebeca stepped back in the room and they both jumped nervously.

"I have brought you some Rondon to eat while you wait," she said as she handed a bowl and spoon to each of them. Gwen looked at it suspiciously and smelled it.

"What is in this?" She asked, wrinkling her nose as she took a sip.

"It is coconut, fish, shrimp, plantain, yam, onions, garlic and other herbs."

Toby was hungry and took a big mouthful while Rebeca described the contents of the delicious smelling meal to the frightened girl.

"It is really good, Gwen!" He looked over at her as she just sat staring at the bowl in her hand. He couldn't tell if the worry on her face was due to not knowing what she was going to eat, or the prospect of heading into the jungle. Probably both, he decided.

"I ... I ... don't think I can eat ... I feel sick at the thought of going off into the jungle." She put the bowl down beside her, and wiped a tear from her eye. A strange tenderness entered Toby, and he tried to comfort her.

"We won't be alone, Gwen," he said, "Rebeca will be with us. She will show us the way to the town so we can get help." He turned to her. "Right?"

"Uh ..." Rebeca let out a breath and pursed her lips, "I can take you part of the way, but it is probably better if I come back here and try to divert Tadeo by sending him the wrong direction. I have some paper from school, and I have drawn you a map to Tudela, where my school is. My teacher, Miss Beddoes will help you. She is very kind. " She paused, then added reassuringly, "It is only a few miles, you will reach there before the sun sets."

"Oh," said Toby. Then, trying to encourage Gwen, he added in an upbeat manner, "Sure! No problem. We can make it in ..." he paused, thinking of his pummelled body, "... in a couple of hours." He forced a grin at her, appearing much more confident than he felt. She half-smiled, then carefully picked up her bowl, and apathetically began consuming the soup.

When they had finished, Rebeca took their wooden bowls and spoon. "I will check on the men," she said, hurrying out the door. Within minutes, she returned with a wide grin. "They are both snoring!" She put a finger to her lips then motioned for them to listen. Sure enough, Toby and Gwen could hear the loud rumbling of Tadeo's henchmen as they slumbered outside from the effects of the intoxicating drink.

"I have brought you a few provisions," Rebeca handed Toby a jute bag, filled with bread, bananas and a leather pouch of coconut water. Unthinking, he grabbed it and carelessly flung it over his shoulder, and in doing so wrenched his aching ribs.

"Ow!" he gasped, causing Emmie to jump up and down on the ledge worriedly, squeaking frantically. Gwen put her hand on his arm.

"Here, I don't have anything to carry, "Let me take the bag." And before Toby could protest, she deftly had the bag off of him and slung over herself. She picked up his backpack, and carefully helped him put it over his tender shoulders. He winced, trying not to let on how much pain he was feeling. Everything hurt.

"Come!" Rebeca waved them out of the hut, and they followed her down the wooden steps into the bright sunshine. Toby stepped gingerly as each step jolted electricity through his battered body.

He glanced nervously around at the small village, noting the women skinning some kind of animal and preparing vegetables. The children were playing happily, laughing and chasing each other, oblivious to Toby and Gwen's impending fate. Several of the women looked up as the three teenagers came out, mildly curious of the visitors.

The village consisted of about twenty huts, all wooden and built on multiple columns. Toby assumed it must flood at least occasionally. Tadeo's men were sprawled on the grass under the shade of a large tree. Although they were completely incapacitated by the sweltering sun and the effects of copious amounts of the cassava, the three teenagers walked as quietly as possible. Even Emmie, who was bouncing along beside Toby, seemed to understand the need for stealth.

Terrified that the men might awaken at any moment, Toby and Gwen's hearts pounded so hard that their ears were ringing as they followed Rebeca, passing within feet of the sleeping figures as she lead them through the village. It was in a fairly open area, on the edge of a river, and behind it was a well-trodden dirt lane, but Rebeca lead them to a barely visible path to the left of the lane and into the woods that surrounded them. Although they were soon immersed in the cool shade of the canopy, Rebeca did not slow her pace until they had walked in silence for about ten minutes along the obscure path. Emmie remained quiet, but kept up with them as she swung her way above them along the branches. Toby wondered how long she would follow them.

The noise under the canopy was almost deafening. Birds whistled and squawked, monkeys chattered and screeched, and many other strange noises that Toby could not identify, filled the air. Toby almost felt inclined to cover his ears as they walked along.

Abruptly, Rebeca stopped and Gwen nearly walked into the back of her. She swung around to face them and took a folded piece of paper out of her pocket. Opening it up, she held it out to them, "Here is the map I have drawn for you. The men will be expecting you to take the main road into town, especially as it is most direct. They would not believe that you would tr … take this path. They will not find you this way." She smiled confidently. Toby and Gwen looked at each other and at the map. "You must not go near these people," she said solemnly, pointing to a crudely drawn hut in the middle of the map. "They do not like white people. They are … an unfriendly tribe and will not welcome you." Nervously, Toby and Gwen looked at each other and took a deep breath simultaneously. Rebeca took a few minutes more to explain all the symbols on the map.

When she finished, Rebeca looked at them both affectionately, a sad smile stretching across her face.

"I would have liked to get to know you both better; to become friends with you. I am sorry to have met you under such … bad circumstances." She embraced them each affectionately. "I will pray for you both." Rebeca looked at them seriously, then added confidently, "Trust God. He will take care of you." Giving them a look of encouragement, she turned and headed off the path into the woods.

"Where are you going?" Gwen asked. "The path leads back that way." She pointed behind them.

"I will find my way to the main road. If the men are awake when I get back, they will see me coming along there and assume you headed out that way." One last wave, and she was swallowed up by the thick undergrowth.

Gwen turned to Toby worriedly. "How are we going to find our way?" He heard the panic rise in her voice, and although he felt anxious himself, he took her shaking hands in his and gripped them gently but firmly.

"We're going to be fine." And with that, Emmie squeaked enthusiastically and swooped down, landing softly on Toby's shoulder.

CHAPTER 8

THURSDAY 5th July – Canada

Benito woke early the next morning, and could not face breakfast. He drank the glass of juice that Doreen gave him, then paced the living room. He wavered from panic at seeing his uncle in person, to worry about Toby, to immense thankfulness at Doreen and Derrick's amazing response. They should have skinned him alive – he certainly deserved it.

"You need to come up with some kind of plan," Derrick said finally. He suddenly realized they were missing a major part of the story. He turned to Benito who stopped pacing as Derrick fixed his eyes on him. "So what was in this package you were supposed to take your uncle, and where is it?"

Benito's clammy hands grew suddenly sweatier and he wiped them nervously on his jeans. His eyes darted from Doreen to Derrick and, sensing another breakdown, they tried to calm him. Doreen smiled, patting the couch beside her and motioned for him to sit down. Derrick sat in a chair opposite, trying desperately to remember the 'grace' he had offered the previous evening. Benito sat down, but his knees trembled and he swallowed several times, then cleared his throat twice. Derrick came close to blowing a gasket as they waited.

"They were diamonds." He took a breath. "I don't have them anymore."

"What?!" Derrick gritted his teeth, pleading with God for patience. Grace. A firm hand to hold him down before he exploded. Doreen looked at Derrick pleadingly, and nodded to Benito encouragingly.

"Go on, Benito," she said encouragingly, her voice belying the absence of the patience she was trying to exude.

Benito explained about the kidnapping of a daughter of some rich man in England and the diamonds being in his bag that would have arrived with Toby. He omitted the part about the few diamonds he had kept back for protection, hidden inside his Nintendo DS.

"The man was told not to go to the police, or his daughter would be killed. He lives somewhere in America, but he was told to get the diamonds to a certain place in England, where I collected them."

Second thoughts began to creep into Derrick and Doreen's mind as the enormity of the venture loomed up before them. Dangers danced before them like silhouettes of haunting figures as they fought back their fears for Toby.

"Like David and Goliath," said Doreen.

"Yes, like David and Goliath." said Derrick. He reached over and took her hands in his. "Just remember who won, honey – and why!"

Benito was lost in thought, chewing his fingernails. "The village leader would probably help you," he spoke up suddenly. They turned to him, waiting for more.

"When we were there last time, I felt that he was not very happy with my uncle, and that he would soon be putting a stop to us going there. I think he is a good man."

"Let's pray he is," Derrick took a deep breath. "Let's pray he is."

CHAPTER 9

THURSDAY 5th July – Nicaragua

Every part of Toby's body protested as they continued walking over the rough path and he began to wonder if they were actually going to make it to the village. Despite his attempt to hide his struggling stride, his pace slowed, but Gwen did not seem to notice. Unknown to Toby, Gwen was glad they were not walking so quickly. She was not used to physical exercise. In fact, she was tiring at Toby's slow speed, and eventually she stopped.

"I need a rest," she puffed, sitting down on a fallen tree that had brown and cream fungus growing out of it like little plates. "Charles, our driver, takes me everywhere. I can't remember the last time I walked anywhere." Toby sat down beside her, happy for the break. He followed Gwen's gaze as she looked down at his purple and green legs that seemed to pulsate pain with every heartbeat. "They look sore." She said softly, running her fingers over his knee. The touch triggered a deep gasp that made his chest complain and he instinctively put his hand on a bandage that covered the worst of his wounds. She smiled teasingly, "Sorry."

"Ya," he said, "They are." He hoped she thought he had jumped because of pain, rather than something else. Though what that was, he was not sure himself. He cleared his throat and changed the subject.

"Do you want a drink?" He took the coconut water out of the bag and offered her some. "Looks like we have to share, so you can go first."

She raised an eyebrow at him, half smiling. "I don't mind your germs." He held her gaze for a moment, then looked away as he took a drink. He had to keep focused. He let a deep breath out through closed lips, and held the map out between them. The swelling in his eye had reduced slightly and he could now see out of it.

Gwen screamed and jumped off the log, frightening Emmie into a screaming frenzy. "Look at the size of that!"

Backing away, she pointed frantically at a large black bristly spider that had been sitting between them, and was now inching its way onto Toby's shorts. He jolted off the log and brushed the spider into the air where it landed several metres away. He was not afraid of spiders, but he had no idea what was poisonous in the jungle. The thing certainly looked it could give you a nasty bite.

"Emmie! It's OK!" he called out, opening his arms as she leapt towards him.

"Emmie?!" Gwen shrieked, "What about me?!" He was about to chuckle, but saw that she was shaking, so he swallowed his smile and went over to her. Putting his arm around her, she curled into him. Emmie started to protest and jumped up on his shoulder barking. They stood there for a few moments, and Toby waited patiently until both of them were calm. Eventually, he let go of Gwen, and turned towards their provisions that were scattered over the ground. Toby picked up what he could, but the water was all gone.

He glanced down at the map that he still had clenched in one hand. If they were where he thought they were, they should not be far from a small river. "Come on, we need to get going."

Reluctantly, she followed as he carried on down the little path and they both stumbled along. Gwen, because she was unfit, and Toby because every one of his injuries told him that he should be resting in bed somewhere instead of floundering around in a jungle. Emmie seemed to understand and leaped back into the branches, following above them. Toby tried to focus on putting one foot in front of the other, frequently checking the map for landmarks or something that would tell him they were heading in the right direction. Nothing. Looking all around him furtively, he lost his footing and tripped on a root, wrenching open one of his wounds as he fell to the ground hard on both knees.

"Are you all right?" Gwen crouched down beside him. Her face grew worried as the blood poured down his shin. Taking the scarf she had tied around her thick gold hair, she wrapped it around his leg, knotting it firmly.

"Thanks," he said sheepishly, scrambling to his feet before she could try to help him. He was embarrassed that he had fallen and he was determined that it would not happen again. He didn't like appearing vulnerable. They carried on along the overgrown path, occasionally being whipped by ferns and branches. Gwen was on a constant look out for any spiders or other unpleasant creatures.

The heat was unbearable and sweat dripped down their bodies. Mosquitoes buzzed around, and Toby finally reached in his bag when he remembered the insect repellent. As he rummaged in his bag, he paused, looking with interest at Emmie, who was on a low branch squashing some kind of caterpillar things and rubbing them into her fur. Whatever they were, the mosquitoes did not like them and swarmed towards Gwen and him. He quickly sprayed them both and was relieved to find it as effective as whatever Emmie was using. He tossed the bottle back in his bag and carefully put it back on.

They continued on, amazed at how warm it was in the shade. Bursts of sun shone through every now and then as gaps in the canopy let through the sweltering rays. Toby and Gwen grew thirstier. And hotter. And more tired.

"I am so thirsty!" complained Gwen, "I cannot go another step without a drink." Toby looked at her, annoyed that she was directing her complaint against him.

"What do you expect me to do?" he said, frowning. He waved his hand around them. "Do you see any water?" She scowled back at him, each of them growing more irritable with every passing moment.

"Oh, what I wouldn't give for a cool glass of iced lemon tea," she said, licking her lips. Automatically, Toby licked his lips.

"Stop that!" he said, "Don't think of drinking. Think of ..." he sighed deeply. "OK, just don't *talk* about it!"

They walked a little further, when Emmie interrupted them by jumping up and down in front of Toby, holding out a small coconut.

"Thanks, Emmie, but how are we supposed to open it?"

"Maybe we can chuck it against a rock," piped up Gwen. Emmie started shrieking at them as they just stood looking at her, and liquid dribbled down her little fingers. Toby shouted.

"It's already open!" He grabbed the coconut from Emmie and turned towards Gwen. "I don't know how, but Emmie has already opened it!" He started to put it to his lips then stopped, and offered it first to Gwen, who took it thirstily, gulping loudly as the liquid ran down her chin. When she had quenched her thirst, she handed it back to Toby who finished off what was left.

"Thanks, Emmie, you're a life-saver!" He bent down and gathered her in his arms. Pleased, she wrapped her furry skinny arms around his neck, and squeaked happily in his ear. "I'll carry you a bit for that!" he stood shakily to his feet, and they recommenced their journey.

It grew dark, and Toby glanced at his watch worriedly, however, it read only 3:10. The sun would not set for another three hours. Splat! A drop of water landed on his watch. Shortly, more drops followed. Toby looked up. Unfortunately, just at that moment, they were in a particularly thin part of the jungle. Before he could say a word, the heavens opened. Gwen started whimpering. He surveyed the area quickly, and spotted a huge tree with a hollow at the base of its trunk. Grabbing Gwen's hand, they ran across and he pulled her in with him. It was a tight squeeze and they sat hunched close together. Toby sighed at the irony that only moments earlier, they were desperate for a drink. Emmie was sitting unperturbed on the branch of a small tree. She had a curious expression on her face, and Toby thought she was probably wondering what they were doing.

"I stink," Gwen said, as the minutes went on and the forced close proximity to Toby in the confined space made her feel self conscious. Toby smiled.

"It's all right, I stink too. So we won't know who smells the worst."

Despite their predicament, Gwen laughed. "Thank you, Toby."

"For stinking?" he joked, knowing what she meant, but feeling uncomfortable with her gratitude.

"For taking care of me." Toby squirmed. They were only together because they were both in danger. He hadn't chosen to be her guardian. He hadn't even liked her at first. He brushed her thanks aside.

"I haven't done a very good job so far." He paused, and held the bottom of her wet blouse. "I couldn't even keep you dry!"

"Well, at least I am not soaking. Just damp." She giggled, glancing up at him with demure emerald eyes and Toby felt himself growing warm.

Just then a ray of light shone outside their cubbyhole, and he scurried out. He stood up and immediately he hurt all over.

He grit his teeth and as he turned to face Gwen he forced a smile. He leaned over, grimacing silently inside, and offered a hand to help her up.

Within a short time, the heat had nearly dried their clothes, and the refreshing rain was quickly a distant memory as the perspiration was again soon trickling down them. Toby grew worried. They hadn't found the river. They hadn't found ANYTHING on the map that Rebeca had made for them.

Gwen grabbed Toby's arm and he twirled around, startled at her sudden grasp.

"What?" he asked, hoping it was not another spider. Instantly he wished it *was* just another spider. He followed her staring eyes. His heart dropped when he saw it: the fallen tree with the plate-like fungus.

CHAPTER 10

Five minutes after leaving Toby and Gwen, Rebeca was out on the main dirt road that linked her village with Tudela, a few miles north. Despite the calm exterior that she had portrayed to Gwen and Toby, her heart was racing as she thought of what the two men would say when they discovered the teenagers gone. If her father or even Tadeo had been there, she would not have worried. She knew that Tadeo would not lay a hand on her, but the two men that Tadeo had brought with him this time had no connection with her or her father, so there would be nothing to hold them back if they decided to hurt her. She slowed her walk. Perhaps Tadeo would get back before her.

She kicked the sandy soil with her toes contemplatively, as she dawdled back home. She looked down at her simple, bright yellow dress. It looked rather tired compared to Gwen's beautiful sapphire blouse and beige cropped trousers. Even her tan loafers, which Gwen had moaned about being 'cheap' were made of a fine, soft leather. The clothes that Rebeca and the others in her tribe wore were made by themselves or acquired from the monthly market in Tudela, where they traded goods. She sighed. She had never been bothered by what she wore before, and she was not really sure why it troubled her now.

"Hey!" A loud deep voice brought Rebeca out of her daydream and she stopped when she looked up and saw the two men stomping towards her. She prayed for Divine protection as she took a deep breath and smiled bravely at them. Asperity. Her word from last week popped into her head. Roughness or sharpness of temper. Definitely asperity.

Another silent prayer, "Please God, save me," as the angry men rapidly closed the distance between them and Rebeca valiantly stood her ground. The taller of the two reached Rebeca first and grabbed her bare arms viciously, shaking her in an uncontrollable rage.

Whack! The back of his big rough hand smacked her cheek hard, gouging her with his ring and wrenching her neck; she stumbled sideways and grimaced in agony as she put her hand to her face, feeling the blood seep through her fingers.

"Where are they?!" He growled at her. He pushed her to the ground and she instinctively curled into a ball with her arms around her head protectively. Like a depraved animal, he kicked her leg with such force, her knee knocked her jaw and Rebeca gasped in pain.

"Stop!" A loud angry voice called out. Rebeca heard the sound of a vehicle approaching and dust flew over her as it stopped suddenly beside her. "You idiot!" Tadeo screamed at the man and punched his ear. He grabbed the man's arm and yanked him away from Rebeca who was still in a tight fetal position, silent tears streaming down her face.

"She let that boy and girl go!" The man defended himself. Tadeo paused, startled by the revelation. He looked down at Rebeca, furious; but the knowledge of what her father would do to him stopped him from hurting her further. He bent down and picked her up as though she were a wounded dog. He placed her on the back seat of the Jeep and jumped in. Turning to the two men, he barked,

"You two will pay if she is seriously hurt!" He started up the vehicle and sped off, shouting over his shoulder, "And you can walk back!"

As he reached the village, Tadeo called out to an older woman who sat by a large pot, preparing vegetables for a soup. It was Rebeca's grandmother, Lucita. She came rushing over as he lifted the girl out of the Jeep and carried her into her hut, placing her gently on the mat, stroking her head caringly. Rebeca was amazed at his guile.

"Abuelita," she opened her arms and her grandmother leaned down into her embrace.

"Que esta bien, mi pequena," her grandmother comforted her.

"She was attacked on the road to Tudela". He would worry later about explanations. "Ire hervir un poco de la planta de serpiente," he said, and he hurried out to boil the snake plant so Lucita could bathe the wounds on her cheek and leg.

Once Tadeo had given Lucita all that she required to tend to Rebeca, he went to find his men to discuss their next course of action. He found them lying under the same tree that they had been under earlier, drinking more casava. He scowled at them and they nervously waited for him to explode.

"How did they escape?!" he seethed through gritted teeth. They looked at each other guiltily and Tadeo glared at their drinks. He knocked them out of their hands. "I can guess! You two are such imbeciles, I do not know why I thought you could be of any use to me!" Sweat was pouring down his brow from both the heat of the day and his temper. "Get up! We will go find them!" He jumped in his Jeep and motioned the men impatiently to follow him.

"Wouldn't you have seen them along the way?" asked the bigger man as Tadeo headed out of the village.

"Nah! They would easily have heard my vehicle coming and could have hidden in the bushes. I will drive a little way past where I found you two halfwits, and then we will walk quickly and sneak up on them."

"I can't see them getting too far after the good going over you gave that boy!" the smaller man smiled, revealing his rotten teeth. He laughed a childish laugh and Tadeo shook his head. He'd have to get rid of these two losers before he headed back to England. How they had been clever enough to escape a criminal record so far, even in Nicaragua, was beyond him. Total and complete luck. Had to be.

After several hours of searching, Tadeo gave up and he returned with his men to the village empty handed and, if it were possible, even more cross. There was just enough light for him to peek in on Rebeca and see her sleeping comfortably with Lucita sitting cross-legged beside her. She looked up at Tadeo and squinted angrily at him. He guessed that Rebeca had told her what had happened. It was time to leave. In the morning they would pack their bags and he would send his men with the Jeep back to the main village and he would walk the little path; she must have sent them that way. It was shorter than the main route, but certainly harder to follow. Rebeca must have had a lot of faith in those two if she thought that they would be able to find their way. Silly child.

He would have to get the diamonds off Benito when he got back to England. It was highly unlikely that Benito would be able to get a flight down to Nicaragua – he wouldn't have the money for a start. Tadeo had been in a rage when he made the call and was not thinking clearly. The four diamonds that Benito had kept back were Tadeo's cut anyway. The rest he had delivered to 'The Boss' when he went to phone Benito. All he needed to do was tie up the couple of loose ends that were lost in the jungle.

"Hmmmm," Tadeo thought to himself, "I could just let them die of natural causes." He chuckled out loud then paused, his mind ticking over. "But then there is a chance that they may find their way out." He felt certain he could find them and deal with them before his flight back to London on Sunday.

"What now?" Gwen's eyes pleaded with Toby to have an answer. Toby was desperate. He had no idea what to do. He looked at Emmie who bounced on the path in front of them, anxious to move on. If only she could talk. She probably knew were everything was in this jungle. He looked at his watch. It would be dark soon. They had to find somewhere to rest for the night. He quickly scanned the area, but there was nothing he could see that would be suitable. He seized Gwen's hand, partly to keep her going, partly to try and calm her, and led her forward. As they walked, he looked upwards. Once again, the thought occurred to him that it was better not to sleep on the ground.

Five minutes later, he spotted it. A huge tree that had been split by perhaps, a lightning bolt, as there was black scorching down the middle. The split stopped about fifteen feet in the air, and while the one side had stayed up, the other had fallen outwards, catching on the branch of another tree. A perfect place to sleep. A thick climbing vine encircled the tree, making the climb easy. Or it would have been, had they not both been so exhausted. Toby's body felt numb, but he climbed ahead of Gwen, and pulled her along behind him, thankful that she was so light.

The wood was a bit rough, so Toby placed his hoodie down to make it more comfortable for Gwen. Remembering her earlier flirtation, Toby glanced at her nervously, but he needn't have worried: Gwen's eyes were already half closed as she sat down on the top and let out a deep sigh. Toby took out a sweatshirt and a waterproof jacket from his backpack and placed them on top of some small branches that hung over them, in case it rained. It wasn't perfect, but at least they wouldn't get soaked.

"Are you hungry?" he asked. She shook her head, too weary to reply. Toby was drained as well, but he was still hungry, so he took a papaya out of the bag that Rebeca had given them and cut it in quarters to make it easier to eat. He sat down beside Gwen and ate it with a handful of nuts that he got from his own bag. When he finished, he tried to make himself comfortable and settled back in a half sitting position against the trunk. Gwen nestled herself against Toby and rested her head against his chest. She leaned hard against his arm and he had to lift it up and put it around her shoulders to make himself comfortable. He felt awkward at first, but Gwen was quickly making soft snoring noises. Pride inched its way into his chest as he thought about their perfect resting place. And as Gwen rested against him he felt like maybe he could take care of her after all. For a moment. Thoughts of just happening upon the tree, and not knowing where to go tomorrow pushed their way through and popped his pride like a slow leaking balloon.

Emmie tucked herself in between Toby and Gwen like a jealous teenager, and Toby chuckled. He gave her a little scratch on her head, then rested his hand on her furry belly and fell asleep.

CHAPTER 11

Toby's eyes shot open. The sound of night-time insects filled the air. But that wasn't what woke him. There it was again! Somewhere between a growl and a low howl, exactly what he heard the first night. What was that? It sounded so close. And again, louder, and more often. Surely it wasn't the jaguar. It sounded like there were a few of them, calling from different parts of the jungle.

Just then, Gwen woke and startled by the noise, grabbed Toby's knee and his heart leaped up into his throat. "What is that?!" she whispered loudly, still clutching his leg. Toby grimaced from her grip.

"Can you let go?" he gasped through gritted teeth.

She released her hold, but tucked herself even closer under his arm, frightened at all the strange noises of the night. The howling continued, and she began to whimper. "What IS that?!" she repeated frantically.

As Emmie still seemed comfortable and unruffled, nestled between the two of them, Toby grew calmer. "I don't know. I heard it the first night I was hear and thought it was a ja…" he paused, not wanting to frighten her. "Well, I wasn't sure, but the noises are in the trees around us, and Emmie doesn't seem frightened, so I wonder if they are monkeys of some kind. At the very least, if Emmie isn't afraid, maybe we shouldn't be either."

"I thought monkeys just chattered and squawked," she replied. He could feel her relaxing beside him, and he spoke calmly, trying to reassure her.

"You know, I seem to recall an animal called a howler monkey. That would make sense. Kind of a haunting noise, isn't it?" Immediately he regretted his choice of adjective as she shivered beside him. They sat in silence, listening to the spooky calls of the strange sounding monkeys – if that was what they were. Eventually, the howling stopped, and the various insect songs filled the air. Adrenalin seeped out of Toby and Gwen, and fatigue began to creep in, as they relaxed back into sleeping positions. Emmie gave a little squawk as if to admonish them for disturbing her and she too, resettled herself.

However, though he was relaxed, he found himself struggling to get back to sleep as various thoughts drifted in and out and then paused over the events of the past few days. "Gwen?"

"Uh huh?" She only sounded half awake.

"What do you think about God?"

"God?" queried Gwen, unsure of what he was asking. "You mean, am I religious?"

Toby shook his head, then realized she couldn't see him. "No." He paused. "Religious is a funny word. I mean, you can be religious about anything, can't you?"

"I suppose so," Gwen said, disinterested. Then, thinking it would stop Toby from talking if she answered, slowly added, "No, I am not religious about God. I guess I believe there IS a God, but I don't ever think about Him. God doesn't affect my life at all."

"But that doesn't make sense," Toby puzzled.

Gwen sighed, wishing she had pretended she was asleep.

"I mean, it is like politics."

Gwen had no idea what he was talking about, but did not reply, hoping he would think she had suddenly dozed off.

"Some people say they aren't 'into' politics, that it doesn't have anything to do with their lives."

"Ya?" Gwen growled softly.

"But politics affect everything you do, from what nutrients are in your food to what the road is like that you drive down. So to say it doesn't affect you, is nonsense."

Gwen was losing what little patience she had. She did not see where he was going and she really did not care. "So?"

"Well, if you believe that God exists; God who created the world and sent His Son to earth to die and then brought Him back to life again," he sorted through his thoughts as he spoke. "Then He has to be involved in everything. I don't think He would go through all that trouble and grief, and then walk off and forget about us. That doesn't make sense. It HAS to matter what you think about Him if you believe He exists."

"Toby, if it will end the conversation so I can sleep, then I change my mind. I don't believe in God, OK? Can I go to sleep now?"

Toby opened his mouth to say more, then changed his mind and let her drift off. He lay awake for a while afterwards, lost in his own thoughts as he stroked Emmie's belly. Like stroking a cat or a rabbit, it was amazingly soothing. And suddenly, so were all the strange night time sounds of the jungle that filled the air. The exertion from the day's walk had taken its toll on the two teenagers and despite the tree being an uncomfortable bed, they both slept deeply.

⟫●⟪

FRIDAY 6th July

They heard Emmie before they were conscious of what the noise was. Toby woke first as Emmie began bouncing on him impatiently. He tittered as she offered him a mango and showed her teeth in an infectious smile. As soon as he took it, she flew off across the branches and was quickly back with another one. She offered it to Gwen, who grabbed it hungrily. She turned to Toby.

"Can you peel this for me?" She asked, holding it back out to him.

Toby raised an eyebrow. "The skin is not that tough, fresh off the tree."

She tilted her head and looked up at him coyly. "Please?"

He shook his head and smirked, but proceeded to cut the mango in half and dig out the stone so she could eat the flesh from the skin. He handed the pieces back to her. "Here you go, princess," he chuckled. Somehow his sarcasm was lost in translation, and Gwen smiled up at him in pleasure.

After a couple more mangoes, and the remainder of the nuts, Toby gathered the items of clothing and placed them back in the bag, then he helped Gwen down to the ground. Not sure of what to do, but not wanting to worry Gwen, he spoke confidently as he held out the map, looking at it like he understood it.

"Right, let's try this again, shall we?" As he hoped, his enthusiastic approach brightened her face and they continued on their journey.

After only a short time, the now familiar sounds of the jungle were interrupted. A girl screaming in the distance pierced the noises that they had grown used to. Or *was* it a girl? It almost sounded like a crazed animal. A few moments later, they could hear what sounded like a few people calling out loudly in a foreign language. Remembering what Rebeca said about the tribe that did not like white people, he pulled Gwen off the trail several metres to the right and ducked behind some bushes, pulling her down with him.

"What are you doing?!" hissed Gwen. "They could tell us how to get to Tudela!"

Toby shook his head. "No Gwen, listen to them!" He commanded sternly.

The crazed girl and the other people were getting quickly closer. "Does that sound like a bunch of people who are going to pause and give us directions?" She pursed her lips, distressed, and Toby was sorry for the harshness of his tone. "How about we follow them?" He nodded kindly and felt like he was encouraging a little child. Gwen sniffed as she nodded in agreement and held Toby's hand nervously in a tight grip. Emmie sensed their trepidation, and snuggled up on Toby's shoulder.

Toby poked his head around a big leaf and watched as they came closer. A girl, probably a couple of years younger than Gwen, was screaming and waving a machete at the group of men and women that were following her. She ran a little way, then turned on them with her large knife, waving it at them as they came closer. At first, Toby thought the people were attacking the girl, but he quickly changed his mind. The small, dark girl had wild eyes and she screamed like she was possessed. The others were shouting, but it sounded like they were trying to calm her down rather than hurt her. Suddenly, as she waved the machete, it slipped from her hand and flew not far from where Toby and Gwen were hiding. Toby ducked instinctively and prayed no one would try to find the offending weapon. He needn't have worried. They saw their chance to seize her and they pounced on the girl who seemed to have the strength of several grown men. Somehow though, they managed to tie her up and it took four large men to carry her as she thrashed about like a wild cat in a net. The group turned and headed back in the direction they had come.

When they were nearly out of sight, Toby grabbed Gwen's hand and pulled her out of the bushes. She started to speak and he put a finger to his lips to quieten her, then motioned in the direction the people had gone. Gwen held on tightly, frightened at what she had just witnessed and the two of them followed, hoping they would be led to a place that would help them. Toby was unsure if the group were from the tribe that did not like white people, and felt it was best to keep hidden from them until he decided if it was safe. If they were the tribe to stay away from, at least he would know where on the map they were.

At first, Toby and Gwen made great efforts to walk quietly, but Toby soon decided that the birds and the insects and the monkeys calling were louder than their steps. The group had stopped calling out to the girl, but she still ranted and screamed like a rabid beast, making it very easy to follow them while staying out of sight.

As time ticked by, Toby and Gwen started growing tired. The girl's screams were growing quieter, and Toby worried they were not keeping up with the group. He tried walking faster, but Gwen began to lag behind.

"Come on, Gwen, we are going to lose them." He turned to face her, and as he did, he noticed a faint *whooshing* sound, like the wind. "What is that?" he asked Gwen rhetorically. She stopped and looked up at him, her face strained, and Toby realized they had been walking a lot faster than the previous day. His injuries seemed to be healing quickly and everything felt less painful today.

"What?" she asked, looking at him blankly, lost in her fatigue.

"That sound, like wind. It sounds like it is coming from up ahead. Come on!" He started to trot ahead, then realized Gwen was still standing in the same spot. He thought quickly, not wanting to get too far behind the people.

"How about I give you a piggy back for a bit?" Her face lit up, and she walked towards him. He gave her his back pack and she slipped it on, then he bent down on one knee, and Gwen hopped on his back. He winced as she wrapped her arms and legs around him tightly. OK, so maybe his injuries did still hurt somewhat after all! However, he said nothing and walked briskly forward. Within a few minutes, the sound was almost deafening, and then they spotted it. A waterfall with a little pool to the right of the path. Toby put Gwen down gently and quickly took out his map. He remembered there was a waterfall somewhere, and he scanned the paper excitedly.

"Here!" he said triumphantly, pointing to the spot on the map. "We're here!"

"So we don't have to keep up with those people anymore?" Gwen asked hopefully.

"No, we don't." As his eyes glanced over the map, his smile faded. They had passed over to another trail. The one that lead to the tribe that Rebeca had said would not welcome them. At least they knew where they were.

"What's the matter?" she asked warily, noticing his change of countenance. He did not want to lie, but decided to not tell her the whole truth.

"We are on the wrong path." He forced a smile, "But at least we know where we are! That is good. We can rest now." He sat down on a rock at the side of the pool and took off his socks and shoes. Gwen slipped off hers and quickly waded in to the welcoming coolness. Toby followed. Gwen stopped when the bottom of her shorts began to get wet. Toby walked past a little further. It was not that deep, probably only up to his waist. They stood in silence for a while as the pleasurable water refreshed their tired feet. Emmie sat on a rock at the edge of the pool, looking at them curiously.

Toby turned with a start as cold water splashed the back of his head and found Gwen grinning mischievously at him, bending over with her hands in the water. He started walking towards her and she scooped both hands up towards him, drenching his face and shoulders. He wanted to be angry, but it felt so refreshing on his skin and Gwen giggled as he playfully scowled, moving faster in her direction, splashing her back. Squealing, Gwen turned and tried to run back to the shore, but her legs dragged in the water and Toby quickly reached her, grabbing her around the waist and tucking her under his arm like a rolled up carpet while she kicked and thrashed with her arms and legs.

"Don't! Put me down! Don't drop me, Toby!" Toby couldn't resist, and pretended he was going to let her fall in the water as he released his grip then grabbed her again. Gwen screamed in response, pounding him teasingly with her fists.

"Ow!" he cried, feigning injury and Gwen burst out laughing.

Suddenly, she stopped moving. "Oh! My bracelet! I've lost my gold bracelet Daddy bought me!" Toby put her down gently on her feet.

"Just stand quietly for a moment to let the water settle," he advised.

They stood in silence, breathing heavily from their playfulness while they waited for the soil to settle under the water. A few minutes later, the water was still enough for them to look for the lost bracelet, and they carefully scanned the clear water.

"Was it very expensive?" Toby asked.

"Well, only a few hundred dollars," she paused. Toby wondered that she could call a few hundred dollars 'only'. "But it was special to me. Daddy took me skiing two winters ago and I twisted my leg quite badly the first day. He was so sweet. He could have just left me in the suite being taken care of by the hotel staff while he carried on skiing the rest of the week – Daddy loves to ski! – but he said he didn't want to leave me, so he hired a wheelchair and took me out each day. We saw it in a shop window in Geneva, and Daddy said the tiny emeralds looked like my eyes, so he bought it for me." She sighed deeply, remembering the trip with her father and how special and loved he had made her feel. "It was the first time he ever took me with him on his skiing holiday. Usually he goes with friends." A tear escaped and ran down her cheek but Gwen was too lost in thought to notice it.

Determined, Toby searched harder and was quickly rewarded by a glint as the dappled sunshine danced below the waters onto the rocky bottom. Gently reaching down so as to not disturb the surface and lose sight of the treasured piece of jewellery, his fingers grasped the bracelet and he handed it to Gwen. Her face immediately illuminated with joy as she took it and examined it carefully.

"The clasp is broken, but the rest of it is fine." She looked up at him gratefully. "Thank you, Toby." She looked down at the bracelet and back up at him tenderly. "This is my most treasured possession. Thank you." She put it carefully in a little pocket at the top of her capris and zipped it up purposefully, then thoughtfully walked out of the pond.

Toby watched her perfect figure as she walked away from him, feeling a deep sadness for this girl. *How ironic*, he thought. She very probably had loads of guys desperate to date her, and here he was alone with her, pitying her.

Finally, Toby headed out of the pool, sitting down on a rock beside Emmie. He took out the map again, while Gwen walked around the edge of the pool absent-mindedly, hopeful that she would soon be back with her family.

Looking at the paper, Toby could see the best way to avoid the unwelcoming tribe was to go back about a mile. He doubted Gwen would be happy about that. The quickest way to get back to the correct path was to carry on another quarter of a mile, to what looked like a clear marker of a small pool, and where they would turn right, and then only another mile to the village. Escape was in sight. Surely if they were just walking by, the tribe would not be bothered by them. Toby made up his mind.

"Come on," he said as he put his socks on. "Another half an hour and we'll be there." Gwen's face lit up and she skipped like a little girl as she shook off her feet, then put on her shoes. "We'll get a drink from the waterfall, first, though."

Gwen followed him around the edge of the pool to the back where the small, but fierce waterfall poured in. Toby held out his hands, catching the cold liquid and gulped thirstily from his palms. He turned to Gwen and realized her arms were not quite long enough to reach the running water, so she had to drink from his hands as he collected the water and offered it to her.

Soon they were happily walking at a brisk pace, both cheered by the prospect of shortly reaching some kind of civilization.

"The first thing I am going to do when I get back to Mommy and Daddy is have a long, hot bubble bath!" Gwen closed her eyes briefly, relishing the thought of relaxing in a deep pile of soothing bubbles that smelled of strawberries.

"Where are your parents?" Toby asked over his shoulder, suddenly realizing he did not know the story of how she was abducted.

"They were on our yacht in the Caribbean when I was snatched by those horrible men. We were moored about a quarter of a mile off of the coast of Antigua and Thomas had just taken me to shore in our little 'runabout' boat."

"Thomas?" interrupted Toby.

"Our butler." She said, as though it were perfectly natural to have a butler. "He had gone into a shop that sold fishing things and I was not interested, so I was waiting outside. I vaguely remember someone coming up close behind me, and something covering my mouth, then I was unconscious. I awoke a while later tied up in the hold of some 'boat'." She said in disgust. "It was a smelly little thing. I could barely breath for the smell of fish." She wrinkled her nose at the memory, then shuddered. "It was really quite frightening. I had no idea what they were going to do to me."

"I'm sure it was," said Toby sympathetically.

"Anyway, just as my head was starting to clear, that Tadeo man appeared and offered me a drink. He seemed quite friendly, but soon after I had finished I was unconscious again, so I suppose he drugged me. The next thing I knew, I woke up in that hut and Rebeca was offering me another drink. Obviously, I was nervous about taking it from her, but in the end thirst took over." She paused a moment thoughtfully. "And she did seem ... well ... *nice*."

"You have an English accent," commented Toby. "Do you ..." he stopped suddenly as screaming entered his ears. It was the crazed girl. He looked at Gwen, remembering he had not told her they would be going close to the danger. She glanced up at him curiously, then heard the girl too.

"Come on, I think the path we want is just up ahead." Toby panicked and began moving at a trot. He heard Gwen breathing heavily behind him as she followed. The small pool came into sight just as he realized he could not hear Gwen panting behind him anymore, and he looked over his shoulder as he kept moving, only to discover she was no longer behind him. He stopped dead.

"Gwen!" he called out loudly in a panic. "Where are you?" He began running back when he heard her call out.

"I'm down this path, I just wanted to have a look."

Just then, Toby found the little path that veered off to the left ... towards the area he wanted to avoid.

"Gwen, stop!" he shouted. Too late, he realized they should have been more quiet. He spotted Gwen just as he saw two angry natives appear in front of her, pointing small but vicious looking spears at them.

CHAPTER 12

"Kisa ou ap fe isit la?" the smaller one growled at Gwen lifting his spear and waving it right in front of her face. Gwen screamed and turned to run.

Without thinking, Toby hollered, "No!" With lightning speed, the larger man propelled his short spear through the air like a missile towards Toby. He darted to the side, but was not quick enough, and the spear entered his left shoulder like a hot knife in butter. Gwen screamed hysterically as Toby's eyes rolled back in his head. He fell to his knees, clutching his shoulder with his right hand as the blood poured through his fingers.

Gwen wailed like a wounded hyena and the shorter man struck her cheek hard to shut her up, as the other man ran towards Toby. Grabbing the end of the spear firmly, he yanked it hard in an attempt to pull it out and Toby shrieked at the pain. The man shouted something that must have been curses, and grabbed Toby's arm to pull him to his feet. The smaller man poked Gwen firmly in the back with his spear, and the two men herded the stumbling teenagers the short distance to their village.

The huts were arranged in a circle with a large open space in the middle. They were all on columns like Rebeca's village, and on the other side was a river. A small group of men gathered round them as they entered the centre. They were all shouting in a strange language and waving spears, machetes and other weapons at them. Tears flowed freely down Gwen's cheeks as she sobbed loudly in terror; her green eyes grew wide and darted around frantically at the crowd, while they pushed and shoved her and Toby towards a huge man dressed more extravagantly than the others in brightly coloured feathers and animal skins. With his impressive looking outfit, Toby guessed that he must be the chief. Toby collapsed as they reached him, and Gwen covered her mouth to stifle a squeal. Toby gasped for breath in agony as he continued to clench his shoulder around the spear.

The chief held up his hand to silence the mob and looked towards a medicine man – sukia – with animal skins draped over his shoulders, crouching beside the crazed girl who had been laid on the ground beside a large fire. She was tied to several small stakes that surrounded her and the sukia was blowing steam over her from a large bowl of hot liquid. He was chanting something over and over in a low, deep haunting voice. He stood, walked two steps, then crouched and repeated his actions. He did this several times until he had completely circled the girl. The whole village began joining in his chants and despite the pain and fear, Toby and Gwen became mesmerized at the scene.

Then, the sukia stopped and stood and the whole village went silent. Seconds ticked by. A prickle raced over Toby's skin as a brisk wind whistled through the village, whipping up the dust from the ground, and then, was gone. An unearthly scream came from the girl's mouth and she began convulsing. No one moved as they watched her writhe and pull at the restraints. Then, unbelievably, she broke free, leapt to her feet and raced out of the village, with several men taking chase. The rest of the people stood and watched for a moment before their attention was drawn back to Toby and Gwen. The chief motioned to the sukia and he came over, stopping by Toby. He stood staring for a moment and then, after speaking a few words to the chief, walked off towards one of the huts. Everyone else slowly went back about their business as the two men that found them, stood guard over Toby and Gwen, and the chief looked on. Gwen huddled close to Toby, shaking with terror. He rested his head on hers trying to comfort her as he gripped on to his shoulder tightly. The blood had stopped running and his whole arm was going numb. He wasn't sure if that was a good thing or not.

Shortly, the medicine man came back with a small bowl and frowned at Gwen, saying something in their native tongue. Gwen just looked at him, confused and worried. The smaller man grabbed her arm and pulled her a few steps away from Toby, then stood watching the medicine man work.

Crouching in front of Toby, the sukia put the bowl beside him and put his hands around the spear where it entered Toby's body. The teenager flinched, closing his eyes while adrenaline began racing through his body at the thought of what the man would do. The medicine man closed his eyes and started chanting again. Different words to the other chant in a different tone – slowly and softly, but determinedly. Then, before Toby could scream 'stop', the man inserted his index fingers deep into his shoulder, grabbed the spear, and it was out. Blood began flowing freely again causing Gwen to screech loudly, and Toby felt himself begin to lose consciousness. The sukia grabbed the pot by his feet and scooped out the moist green mush and slapped it on the wound, pushing some of it in. He held his hands over the wound and began chanting again for several minutes.

Expecting blackness, Toby was surprised that he was still conscious and he let out a slow, deep breath. As he did, he felt like he had just blown up several balloons. Light headed, Toby looked over at Gwen and tried to focus. He smiled goofily at her and began swaying gently as he felt as though he was being filled with helium. The sounds around him began to fade and he started to giggle. Gwen smiled worriedly at him, and he giggled louder. All he could hear was the sound of his own laughter as he began to float slowly upwards, his back to the sky. He looked down at Gwen, at the men, at the village, still laughing, his limbs dangling beneath him. With much effort, he managed to turn over and looked up at the clouds. Colourful birds flew by squawking, whistling, cooing joyful songs, and Toby joined in with them, surprised at the bird-like sounds that came from his lips. One large, multi coloured parrot landed on his stomach. Toby started floating downwards from the weight.

"Hello, Toby," the bird said, in a deep growly voice, his black eyes staring at him.

"Get off, you are making me sink!" Toby replied, as though it were perfectly normal to be conversing with a parrot. The bird suddenly smiled an evil grin, and Toby grew worried when he saw razor sharp teeth. The bird jumped onto his chest and poked his cheek with his beak.

"I'm going to peck out your eyes!" the bird hissed at him and jumped on his face.

Toby screamed and tried to brush the bird off, and as he did, the brightly coloured feathers turned black and came out, floating around him. The more he swiped at the bird, the more feathers came out, until Toby was surrounded in masses of black feathers. Finally, the bird was sitting on him, without one feather left. It let out a horrible ear piercing shriek, started smoking, and was reduced to a pile of ash on Toby's stomach. As he swept off the ash, the feathers disappeared, and Toby started drifting upwards again, slowly starting to relax in the warm sunshine.

Toby continued to rise, and slowly, drifted into a small thick cloud. Suddenly, he was soaking from the moisture, and he grew colder from his wet clothes and the surrounding dampness. He began to shiver uncontrollably until he was convulsing like the crazed girl. He panicked as he was unable to stop the convulsing, and he thrashed about, foaming at the mouth like a rabid dog.

Then, just as he floated above the cloud into the warmth of the sunshine, his convulsions relented and he hung limply as he rose ever higher. And higher. And higher. He struggled to breath as he felt the air growing thinner. As each breath became more of a gasp, his heart pounded heavily. He grew colder. When would he stop? How far would he float? Would he be able to get back down to earth? He tried to shout but no sound came out of his mouth. In fact, it was deathly quiet all around him. Like a vacuum.

The air grew warmer, until it was the same temperature as his body. His breathing returned to normal. But he was still going upwards, faster now into the blackness of space. Slowly, Toby started to relax again and he found he could go in any direction he chose, like he was swimming. The wound on his shoulder was gone, and he pulled himself easily along in a breast stroke. Complete silence surrounded him, more complete than he had ever experienced, and he looked down at the earth, now a small blue ball by his feet. Strangely, though, he was no longer frightened.

Toby looked up and saw the moon growing closer and closer. He swam faster until he felt a gentle pulling towards its surface, and he stopped his movements, allowing himself to drift closer and closer, slowly downward until he landed gently on his feet, dust floating lazily upwards from the surface. He bent down and scooped up some dust in his hands, letting it run through his fingers, and as he did, the dust turned into thousands of miniature scorpions. He tried to shake them off, but they quickly grew bigger and bigger, piercing him over and over. Panic grabbed hold of him again.

"Help!" he tried to shout as he ran, but no sound came out of his mouth. Desperately he tried to brush the creatures off of him. As he continued to run, his breath became more and more laboured. His feet struggling to move forward and Toby stumbled and fell, rolling in the dust. He couldn't stop himself as he rolled to a crater and over the edge. Down, down he tumbled and bounced, wincing in expectation of pain, but feeling nothing.

Hitting the bottom, he stopped dead. He looked down at his body. The scorpions were gone and his skin was unblemished. He looked up at the steep sides. How would he get out?! Some distant stars twinkled down at him. He lay there, his breaths growing slower as he rested in the dust.

"Toby." A deep, warm, comforting voice: "I am here." A bright light blazed in front of him and the heat was almost unbearable. He lifted his hand to shield his face, and the light was gone. The stars disappeared and everything went black. Everything began spinning, slowly at first, then faster. Toby instinctively put his hands down to steady himself, and he closed his eyes tightly as he spun around and around.

"Toby!"

He opened his eyes to see Gwen hovering over him. One man grabbed her and pulled her back as Toby tried to steady himself. His hands firmly gripped the grass on which he sat. He was no longer spinning, but he had no strength to move and he fell onto his back where he lay, staring up at the sky.

The sukia shouted something to the man holding Gwen, and he handed him a machete. Gwen screamed as the man waved the long knife at her head. Wrenching her hair, he took the weapon and began hacking indiscriminately. As she struggled, he cut into her ear and though only a small wound, blood oozed out and down her neck. She stood still as he chopped, terrified that the next chop might cut more deeply. Short, sharp whimpers coming out with each swipe as he pulled at her golden hair.

When he was finished, he let go of Gwen and scooped up the mound from the floor, handing it over to the medicine man. The sukia took it and walked over to the stakes. Toby saw that the deranged girl had been once again retrieved and tied to the stakes in the ground. This time she was motionless. He thought she was unconscious, but her eyes were open, and he wondered if she had been drugged as she stared without blinking.

Taking Gwen's hair, the sukia put it in a pot over the fire, and waited until it was burnt into an ash. He took the ash and scraped some of it into a small cup that had other ingredients in it, and stirred it with a spoon. He took the cup, and walking towards the girl's head, he nodded to a man who ran over to her side and held her head. Four other men held her arms and legs as she began to struggle, and the sukia poured the mixture from the cup into the girl's mouth. She tried to spit it out, but the man who held her head covered her mouth and squeezed her nose until she swallowed the horrific looking 'medicine'. She closed her eyes and stopped moving. Everyone waited for several minutes, but still she didn't move. Eventually, all but the man who had held her head, moved away. He bent down, untying the ropes that bound her, then lifted the girl in his arms and carried her into one of the huts, looking down at her with the obvious love of a father.

The chief looked at Toby and Gwen. Toby was still lying on his back, and Gwen had been left sitting in a crouched position, crying softly as she held her shorn head in her hands. Her ear had stopped bleeding, but her neck and hands were stained red. Toby wished he had the strength to reach up and hug her tightly, but he could not lift a finger. He closed his eyes, giving in to the sleep that beckoned him.

CHAPTER 13

FRIDAY 6th July – Nicaragua

Toby awoke with a start. The sun had begun its descent in the sky, but he was uncomfortably hot. He was lying where he had fallen asleep, but his hands and feet were bound. Gwen was sat on the steps of a hut across from him trying to be inconspicuous, but many of the younger villagers were hovering around her, touching her skin and her hair curiously. She kept trying to shoo them away, but they kept coming back. Gwen's eyes were full of tears, and she looked thoroughly miserable.

Over the fire, a large animal, probably a deer, was being cooked on a spit that one of the children kept turning every fifteen minutes or so. A pot of something, perhaps vegetables of some kind, was bubbling away on the edge of the fire. Toby's stomach growled loudly and he wondered if they would get any of the food. At least it was not something horrible like bat or monkey. He had heard that some indigenous people liked that sort of thing.

Just then, he saw a girl come out of the hut and over to Gwen. It looked like the mad girl. Could it be? She seemed perfectly normal now. She touched Gwen's hair and smiled at her, saying something he could not understand. She tried to hold Gwen's hands, but Gwen pulled away and scowled at the girl. Toby wondered if she were thanking Gwen for her hair. He was not sure Gwen recognized her, but he doubted it would matter. She looked over and saw Toby was awake. A big smile brightened her face and she wiped her eyes as she came rushing over and sat on his left side close beside him on the ground.

"They won't leave me alone, horrible things!" she pouted. Toby half smiled at her, amused.

"I doubt they have ever seen anyone with such light skin or blond hair. My guess is that if the tribal leaders do not like westerners, the younger ones have probably never seen anyone with your colouring before. I'm not as dark as they are, but you would certainly be unique to them."

"I don't care," she said crossly. "I don't want their greasy little dirty, horrible hands touching me! Who knows how clean they are? I doubt they've ever seen a bar of soap. I could catch some nasty disease!"

The children seemed to be wary of Toby for some reason, and did not come near Gwen as she sat next to him. Perhaps after his bizarre episode with the sukia's medicine, they thought he had what that girl did.

"How is your shoulder?" she asked.

Surprisingly, it was just a little numb now. Whatever that medicine man had treated him with was amazing. He should patent it. Though he was not so sure about the hallucinogenic side effects.

"OK," he replied.

"I was worried about you," she said suddenly, leaning into him closely, resting her head on his uninjured shoulder, and a little tingle ran through him as he felt her breath on his neck.

"You started laughing like a weirdo, then your eyes went blank and you went limp for a while. After that, you started shaking and convulsing. I thought you were having a fit or had whatever that girl had! Then you went limp again before you started rolling around on the ground screaming that you were falling."

"Crazy dream," he said simply "I guess there was some kind of drug in the poultice he used." He thought about the voice and the presence at the end of the experience. They seemed very different than the rest of it; almost real.

"But ..."

"But what?" she looked up at him.

He was not about to tell her he thought God had spoken to him. She would think he was nuts; *he* thought he was nuts!

"Oh, nothing."

One of the older men went over to the roasting deer, and poked it with a machete. A little pink juice dripped out. He nodded to another man, and they lifted the deer off the fire and placed it on a large flat rock that lay beside it. A few minutes later, the first man was hacking chunks off with his machete and people were coming up and taking the pieces. The chief had the first, biggest piece, then the older men went next, and then after them, the women and children. The man sliced off two chunks and gave them to the child that had been turning the meat, saying something to him and pointing to Gwen and Toby. The boy took the pieces and walked over to Gwen and Toby.

He said something to them in their foreign tongue and smiled shyly at them as he held out the meat. Toby took a piece eagerly with his bound hands, but Gwen looked down at the boy's dirty hands and made a face. The boy started to turn, and Toby grabbed the other piece and thanked him, nodding his head and smiling. The boy returned his smile, then trotted off to get his own food.

"Gwen," he reprimanded her, "You have to eat something. Who knows when we will get something else. Aren't you hungry?" As if in reply, her stomach growled, and she reluctantly took the piece of meat from Toby, nibbling at it gingerly. Toby tucked in and it did not take him long before he was finished. He couldn't remember when anything had tasted so good. Gwen ate only half of her piece, and was about to throw the rest on the ground when Toby stopped her.

"I'll finish it, I'm still hungry."

Before Toby finished, a woman came along with a pot of vegetables of some kind, and offered some to Toby. She looked at his ties, and reached in, grabbing a couple of pieces and gave them to him. Gwen hurriedly took some herself, before the woman could touch them.

"At least no grubby hands have touched this," she said happily.

When they had finished, Toby turned to Gwen. "Would you be able to help me move under this hut a bit? I am getting really warm and could do with a little shade." With a little wriggling from Toby and some struggling from Gwen, they managed to get him under the wooden house and in some shade. Toby sighed with relief.

"This heat is really tiring," he said and Gwen nodded. He lay on his right side and tried to make himself comfortable on the grass. Gwen lay down beside him, and soon they were both asleep.

CHAPTER 14

FRIDAY 6th July – Doreen and Benito / Nicaragua

The trip down to Nicaragua was long, as there was a five hour stop over in Houston, Texas. Neither Doreen or Benito could sleep much, and they arrived exhausted at 2:00 Friday afternoon. Doreen had arranged to meet Joe in a central area of the airport by some head monuments that she had seen on the internet. It was not a big airport, and after quickly going through customs, they soon met up with a frantic Joe. He looked similar to Toby, with his dark eyes and hair, though he had filled out his six foot two inch frame and was solid from the sport that he did.

"What's going on, Aunt Doreen?" He queried as he gave her a big hug. He turned to Benito who had shrunk back in anticipation of Toby's brother's reaction to him. "And who is this? Uncle Derrick said there had been a mix up and Toby had accidentally gone to Nicaragua! How on earth did that happen?! Toby is not stupid, he would not have gotten on the wrong plane." He kept glancing at Benito, who was hiding behind Doreen, waiting for an explanation that Benito was unwilling to offer. Doreen instinctively put a protective arm around Benito, fully aware of Joe's plausible reaction and Benito sank into her protective stance.

"I don't know why you did not call the embassy to help us! And why did I need to put my stuff in a back pack?" Joe grew suspicious of Benito's silence, and turned on him in fierce anxiousness. "Can't you speak?!" Doreen put her hand on Joe's arm to calm him.

"Let's just sit down, and I will explain." They found a bench, and Benito immediately sat on the outside, so Doreen was between him and Joe. She took Joe's hands and asked him to just compose himself as best he could, and listen without interrupting. Just as she had nearly finished, Joe leaped up and reached over Doreen, grabbing Benito by the collar, and shouting at him.

"You horrible little coward!" Benito hung in Joe's strong arms like a frightened puppy, and Doreen struggled to get him to let go as the passing people began to stare.

"Put him down, sweetheart," Doreen pleaded quietly. "I know you are angry, but this isn't going to help Toby." She was no match to remove him physically, and had to rely on Joe to finally see reason. Unwillingly, Joe let go and Benito dropped to the floor like a pile of dirty laundry. Joe just stood glaring at him, breathing heavily and trying to gather his thoughts.

"So what is the plan?" he said at last, still glaring at Benito. He looked at Doreen expectantly.

"We need to hire a guide to take us to this village," she began. "We decided it was best that we leave Benito just outside the village and try to speak to the chief, Lucio, alone, first. We need to establish if Toby and this girl are still there, and where his Uncle Tadeo is." She motioned towards the boy that sat crumpled at their feet. "Benito said that Lucio will help us. We do not know if Toby will still have the diamonds, so we need to find out where they are, to see what bargaining tools we have."

"That's not much of a plan," said Joe, glancing down at Benito.

"It's all we have at the moment, Joe. We'll just have to play it by ear, and trust God to guide us." As she said that, Joe's heart softened slightly and he held out a hand to Benito who flinched, thinking Joe was going to strike him.

"I'm not going to hit you, you pathet..." he stopped himself, trying to imagine what Benito had lived with when he was with his uncle. "Come on, get up." He yanked the frightened boy to his feet unceremoniously. "Let's go find someone who can take get us to this village."

It would take a few hours by car and would have been quicker using the helicopter company that Tadeo used – advised Benito. However, the cost was too much, and Doreen had decided they would just have to take the long way.

An hour later, they were all piled in a Jeep. The first hour, they travelled quite fast down a paved road and the time passed quickly, but at a small town, they turned off the tarmac and continued the journey bouncing along a well-used, but rough, dirt road. As the vehicle could not travel nearly as fast now, they had little wind to cool them off, and the hot sun beat down on them mercilessly.

Benito looked out at the landscape as it moved slowly along his view. The road wound its way through a valley with a mixture of trees and open fields. He was uncomfortable in every way possible. Sweat was trickling down his forehead because of the intense heat of the sun, and there was not a breath of wind. Not even from the movement of the vehicle that seemed to be bouncing more than it was moving forward and his body was continually bombarded by jolts.

Benito thought about his uncle and the rage that he would be in, and the sick feeling in his stomach grew with each minute that passed by. He glanced over at Joe who sat across from him in the back seat scowling, and thought about this 'grace' that Doreen had tried to explain to him on the plane journey. He still did not quite get it. God sent His Son to die and rise again so that if he, Benito trusted in Him to take the punishment for his sins, he could go to heaven, even though he did not deserve it. That was grace. He glanced out the window and then back at Joe, wondering how that related to him. Joe had not killed him ... yet. He guessed that was grace, but he could not figure out how the two things were related. Doreen said that he had to 'accept' the gift of grace, otherwise it was useless, but Benito could not fathom how he could accept a gift that he could not see.

An exceptionally large bounce knocked everyone out of their thoughts and there were *oompfs*! from all of them, especially from Joe who hit his head on the roof of the jalopy.

"Are you two boys all right back there?" Doreen turned her head from the front, frowning at the unconcerned driver as she did. Joe was rubbing his head.

"I am fine, Aunt Doreen," he said. Then added, "Well, I think I am. My brain feels like it has been knocked around my head but I am still conscious, so I guess that is a good thing." He looked at Benito and half smiled. Benito smiled back nervously, waiting for an attack.

"I'm sorry, Benito." Joe said finally, and Doreen nodded approvingly, turning back her focus to the road ahead, hoping to be able to warn them next time there was a major bump.

Benito looked at Joe suspiciously. "Sorry for *what*?" he asked Joe.

Joe took in a deep breath and let it out slowly before answering. "I am sorry for being so nasty to you at the airport."

Benito raised an eyebrow. He had been expecting Joe to do him some serious injury at first chance when Doreen was out of view. He had never expected an apology. This family was truly odd. A good odd. But odd, nonetheless.

Curiosity got the better of him, and Benito asked, "Why?"

"Why am I sorry?"

"Uh, ya."

Then, Benito added hastily in case Joe changed his mind, "Not that I am not grateful you are sorry, of course."

Joe looked over at the boy cowering in his seat and sighed. He really was a weasely, pathetic creature. "I'll be honest with you, Ben," Joe hesitated as he pursed his lips, and Benito felt tears well up in his eyes. Only his mom ever called him Ben. Joe rubbed his eyes and sighed at the sight of what he considered even more weakness in the boy as he saw his moist eyes.

"It is not because I like you. I don't. I think you are a ..."

"Joe!" Doreen admonished her nephew strongly, looking over shoulder frowning, and Joe felt a small pang of guilt at his pride. Pride in his own strength of character.

"I forgive you because God forgave me my sins. Because He first loved me and forgave me, I want to show that love and forgiveness to others." Benito looked even more confused.

"So you want to show me love, even though you don't like me?"

"I didn't say I was perfect, I said I was forgiven!" Joe chuckled despite the worry for his brother that pervaded his chest.

Benito stared at Joe, unsure, and Joe tried again. "Look, when you are a Christian, you don't always *feel* forgiveness to another person. You are so grateful that God has decided to wipe out your sins and give you a clean slate, sometimes you just forgive people because you know they are sinners like you are, not because you *feel* forgiveness for them in your heart."

"Oh ... I see." Said Benito slowly, trying to process this new way of looking at things in his mind. "So, does God forgive me, too?"

"Yes. God forgives you for everything, if you are truly sorry."

"Why?"

"Because He loves you. For no other reason than that. He loves you."

"God loves me?"

Joe nodded his head, and Doreen smiled to herself in the front.

"Wow."

"Ya," Joe agreed. "Wow."

An hour and a half later, the driver finally stopped. The trees had grown quite thick now and they could just see the corner of one of the huts. They all grabbed their bags and climbed out of the jalopy, glad to be out of the uncomfortable vehicle and standing still.

Doreen turned to the driver. "Will you come back for us on Tuesday?" she requested.

"No entiendo," he shrugged and held up his hands. Doreen sighed. In their haste, she had not even realized the man did not speak any English, as Benito had done all the talking, telling him where they wanted to go.

Benito came to their rescue, grateful that he could actually do something positive, and spoke to the man in Spanish, who nodded, then said something back, laughing as he hopped in the Jeep and drove off.

"Is he coming back? Why did he laugh?" asked Doreen worriedly.

So much for the rescue. Benito hung his head and spoke softly. "He said he was on holiday next week and he would pass the message on..."

Joe lifted his hand to strike Benito, but Doreen caught it and brushed it away, shaking her head at him. "We'll worry about the return journey later." She turned to Benito, who could not raise his face to look at them. "It is okay, honey." Joe opened his mouth to speak, then shut it when Doreen frowned at him. Turning back to Benito, she added, "Wait here while we go see if we can find this Lucio fellow." With that, she took Joe forcefully by the arm and headed towards the village.

Rebeca was just slowly walking around the corner of her hut, her thoughts concerned with Toby and Gwen, when she saw the two strangers walking towards the village. Her leg was still quite sore, but she managed to walk without limping. As the man and woman got closer, Rebeca smiled. The man must surely be related to Toby, they looked very similar. His family must have come to rescue him. Her smile faded as she realized they probably assumed he would still be there in the village, safe. Her thoughts raced as she wondered how best to explain. She did not know how much they knew of the situation.

When they were close enough to Rebeca, the woman spoke. "Do you speak English?"

She continued when Rebeca smiled and nodded her head. "Yes."

"My name is Doreen, and this," she motioned to Joe, "is Joe. We are looking for my nephew, Toby. We were told he would be here and that we should speak with the chief, Lucio." The woman spoke confidently, but smiled warmly and Rebeca liked her instantly.

At the sound of his name, Chief Lucio poked his head out of the hut where he had been resting from the heat of the afternoon, waiting for the women to cook the evening meal.

"I am Lucio," he spoke with authority, but looked hesitantly at Rebeca for help with translation. His English was limited.

Lucio put his arm protectively around Rebeca's shoulders when he reached her. He was still very angry about what had happened to her when he was gone, and was concerned for her safety with the appearance of these strangers.

Rebeca spoke to her father in Spanish and his face softened. He had been feeling guilty about his part in the boy and girl's predicament. Rebeca turned to Doreen who waited patiently for a reply.

"I am sorry to tell you that he and Gwen are no longer here." Doreen and Joe's hearts sunk and their hopeful faces fell at the news.

"Where are they?" asked Joe, louder than necessary and Doreen shot him a warning look. He reluctantly let Doreen continue.

"Do you know where they are?"

Rebeca could barely bring herself to speak as she pointed to the dense growth behind the village. Tears formed in her eyes, and although his heart softened at the sight, Joe grew even more alarmed for the safety of his brother.

Rebeca barely spoke above a whisper as she replied, "Yesterday, I showed them the path to take to the town, Tudela; but we just had word today from some men in our village who have been out hunting. Two white teenagers have been captured by the Alejate tribe."

"Show us where!" shouted Joe, "We have to go save him. What will they do to them?"

Lucio and Rebeca spoke to each other urgently in Spanish, before Rebeca replied. "We have been trying to think of the best way to get them back." She did not want to tell Toby's family exactly what might happen to him and Gwen. "They are not an agreeable tribe, so my father was deciding if there was something we could use to trade with them. We do not wish to stir up animosity between them and our tribe. They leave us alone if we do not bother them." Sensing compassion and reasoning in Doreen, she looked at her directly and added gently, "My father has our tribe to think of, as well."

Doreen and Joe stood in stunned silence at the revelation. Doreen's strong faith was wavering and she suddenly looked very pale. Rebeca stepped towards her and took her hand.

"Come, you must both be very weary and hungry. We can do nothing for the moment. Come by the fire and rest. The stew will be ready soon."

Doreen suddenly remembered Benito. "There is a boy back there," she waved in the direction from where they had just come. "His name is Benito." Her eyes were glazed as she tried to remain coherent. "He was concerned that his uncle would hurt him."

Rebeca explained to her father, and his face clouded over, answering her angrily.

Rebeca translated. "We know Benito. I will go get him. My father says that Tadeo is gone and will not be back ... ever. He has forbidden him to set foot in our village ever again."

Lucio motioned for Joe and Doreen to sit by the fire where tribe members were gathered, watching them with curiosity. They were unsure of their appetite, but sat down obediently.

Shortly, Rebeca returned with a very worried-looking Benito. She had explained to him about Toby and Gwen, and Benito was wondering if this forgiveness thing would hold out.

Doreen patted the ground between her and Joe, and after a slight hesitation, Joe nodded. Benito walked over and his stomach growled as he sat down.

There was plenty of food to go around, as the hunters had killed a large deer. Rebeca and her grandmother dished out the venison and vegetable stew into wooden bowls, and passed them around. Despite their anxiousness for Toby, Doreen and Joe found they were hungry, and were soon joining the rest of the tribe as they consumed the food. They probably would have found it quite delicious had worry not permeated their stomachs.

By the time everyone was finished, the sun had set and darkness settled around them. Night sounds began to fill the air. A roaring began in the nearby jungle and Doreen looked nervously in that direction. Rebeca touched her shoulder and reassured her. "It is only a howler monkey. They make a strange noise, but they will not hurt you."

"I thought it might be a jaguar," said Joe. "Are there jaguars in Nicaragua?"

"There are jaguars, yes," Doreen's eyes grew wide and Rebeca hurried to assure her. "But they are not interested in us. There are many deer here and jaguars much prefer them."

Doreen frowned deeply at the thought of Toby in the jungle with jaguars and unfriendly tribes and who knew what else?

"Doreen," Rebeca spoke softly.

"Yes?"

"I believe God will protect them." Doreen squeezed her hand gratefully as an instant bond between them surfaced. Rebeca glanced at Joe, and he nodded his head, looking at her deeply. She was an ordinary-looking girl but something about her intrigued him, drawing him in. Rebeca lowered her eyes as he stared at her, and she turned away to gather up the dishes.

Joe stood. "Let me help you." He was amazed at how she managed to pile so many dishes expertly in her arms, compared to his feeble offering, and he followed her to the edge of the river, where they rinsed everything they had gathered.

"How come you speak English so well, compared to everyone else around here?" Joe asked curiously, as he followed her up the stairs to her hut and helped her put the dishes in the corner.

Rebeca explained to Joe all that she had relayed to Toby when she first met him. When she got to the part about her mother, Joe's heart melted and he looked into her soft intelligent eyes.

"How awful for you," he said.

"I am okay, now," she said quietly, not wanting his sympathy but enjoying his attention. He was very much like Toby, though much more self assured. Toby. She prayed he was all right. She prayed God would protect him and Gwen. The Alejate tribe had been known to sacrifice people they had captured to their gods to try and appease them and release their young people of the Grisi Siknis.

"Come, I will show you and Doreen to the hut where you will sleep. You must be tired, I am sure."

Joe nodded, suddenly feeling quite exhausted from the all traveling and the worries. "Yes, I am sure Aunt Doreen could do with some rest."

Rebeca showed the two of them to the hut that Gwen and Toby had been in. She shuddered at the treatment that they had experience and worried afresh about their safety.

After seeing that Doreen and Joe were settled in, Rebeca returned to her own hut and lay down, though she was not tired. Her heart was very heavy and she lay there for a while praying before she finally fell into a fitful sleep.

CHAPTER 15

Early SATURDAY morning 7th July – Alejate tribe / Toby and Gwen

The drug in the poultice drew Toby into a deep sleep, and he did not wake until it was dark. His wrists and feet remained tied and he was lying on his side on the ground, still under the hut. Gwen was now bound as well, and lying next to him. A group of men, women and children were dressed in brightly coloured feathers and skins, and they were dancing around the fire singing loudly. Others were sat watching while they ate and drank. He wondered if they were drinking fermented casava, since they all appeared inebriated; even the children. They looked like they were having a celebration, he thought, perhaps for the crazed girl who had been healed.

A soft squeaking came from behind him and he rolled over to face Emmie. She jumped on him and wrapped herself around his neck. He started coughing. He ached all over – probably from lying on the ground in such an uncomfortable position.

"Not so tight, Emmie!" he said quietly, not wanting anyone to notice. He was not sure what they would do to her.

"Toby?" mumbled Gwen. "My wrists and ankles hurt."

"Mine too," he answered.

He looked at his watch. "It's two thirty! Don't these people sleep? Even the kids are awake, can you imagine? My parents wouldn't let me stay up that late when I was a kid." He laughed quietly, thinking about his own parents. A pang hit him as he pictured all of his family and he suddenly missed them terribly.

"My parents let me do whatever I want," said Gwen, almost sadly. "I sometimes wish they would have made rules.

127

It's almost like they don't..." she broke off, and Toby turned to look at her. Tears welled in her eyes.

"Care?" he finished questioningly. She nodded and Toby continued compassionately. "Of course they care, they sent those diamonds for your ransom, didn't they?"

She sighed, "Oh, that wasn't much, considering what money Daddy has." She swallowed hard, "He'll probably find a way to write it off for tax purposes, anyway."

"Do you have any brothers or sisters?"

"No," she sighed even deeper. "Mommy said she couldn't bear to be pregnant again because she gained a lot of weight and it took her a long time and a lot of effort to get rid of it." She closed her eyes for a moment before adding with pride, "Mommy is the most amazingly beautiful woman I know."

Toby looked at Gwen's forlorn face, studying it in the light dancing from the fire. Even with her horrific haircut, he had never seen anyone so stunning.

"If she looks anything like you, I am sure she is." He said genuinely.

She frowned and looked at him through squinted eyes, sure that he was teasing. "Funny." She said curtly, "With this hair and no makeup?"

"Gwen," he said, surprised that she didn't seem to know, "You're naturally beautiful. You don't need any make-up."

She still was not completely convinced, but as Toby looked at her seriously, she relented. "Really? But I've worn make up for as long as I can remember. Mommy said it was important to always look my best."

"Really!" he replied, assuring her firmly.

She smiled gratefully at him and leaned over, kissing him gently on his cheek. Toby was glad it was dark, as he felt his face grow warm from the touch of her soft lips. "Thank you, Toby."

Just then, Emmie moved to his wrists, and started pulling at the rope that bound him.

"I don't think you are strong enough, Emmie, but thanks for trying," he said softly. Gwen yawned quietly behind him, and he yawned in response. Very soon, the two of them were fast asleep.

The sky was just starting to get light when Toby felt a tugging at his feet, and as he reached out, he realized his wrists were free. He looked down at his feet, and saw Emmie chewing through the ropes. Wow! She must have sharp teeth, he thought. He was glad she liked him! Two minutes later, his feet were free as well. Toby turned over to Gwen and saw she was still sleeping. He shook his wrists and wriggled his fingers until the feeling came back, then began to untie Gwen.

"What…?" she called out as she woke.

"Shhhh!" he put his finger to his lips and continued in a whisper, "The whole village is still asleep. They probably are sleeping quite deeply, if they were drinking what I think they were drinking, but we don't want to chance them waking."

"How did you get untied?" She looked at the chewed ropes that lay beside him. "Did you use your knife?" He shook his head.

"Emmie chewed me free. I don't know where my bag is." He suddenly thought of the diamonds in the Nintendo. He finished untying Gwen and stood up, stretching his arms and legs and looking around as Gwen wriggled her wrists and ankles to get the movement back. He finally spotted his backpack on the ground where the sukia had treated him. In all the excitement of their capture and the crazed girl, it must have been forgotten. He hurried over and picked it up. He swung it over his right shoulder and he grimaced as he lifted his left arm through the strap. It was still quite stiff, but he was grateful that he could feel it at all. The picture of the spear sliding into him flashed before him and he thanked God for the healing poultice of the medicine man.

He looked over to Gwen. She was just rising to her feet, and ran her fingers through what was left of her hair. She didn't see him watching her and she smiled to herself as she recalled Toby's words of compliment, slowly sliding her hands down her cheeks and marvelling at the revelation. He turned away, not wanting to embarrass her.

"Come on," he called out quietly over his shoulder, "Let's go!" Emmie scampered past him, and Gwen hurried along behind, as they headed back into the jungle, hoping to at last find their way to the village where Rebeca's teacher would help them get back home.

They had only gone a few metres into the trees when they heard shouting from the village. They were awake! Toby broke into a run. "Come on!" Toby called out needlessly as panic entered Gwen and she raced along behind him.

Everything in Toby wanted to run faster, but he knew Gwen could not keep up, so he slowed his pace as he heard Gwen gasping for air. They reached the small pool, and Toby turned left. Gwen started to slow, but the thought of the men with their spears spurred her on again and they raced along for a while before she stumbled and stopped, calling out to Toby,

"Toby! I ... can't ... go ... on ..." she took a gulp of air, "at this ... pace ...!" He reached out for her hand.

"Just a little further," he pointed ahead, "the undergrowth gets really thick up there. We'll hide off the path a bit in case they come down this way." Toby darted into a gap and headed off the path, then went parallel with it until the ferns grew so thick you couldn't see through them. He crouched down and Gwen collapsed next to him, her chest hurting from lack of oxygen. Emmie scurried under the ferns with them, and they sat quietly, breathing heavily. She looked at them curiously, but made no noise as she snuggled onto Toby's lap.

They sat silently for a few minutes, then Toby looked at his watch. "We'll wait another twenty minutes," he whispered. Gwen nodded thankfully, glad for the time to rest.

They listened to the noise of the jungle: squawks and chatters and squeals and odd noises echoing through the trees. Emmie seemed to be listening as well, and Toby wondered if she was missing her family. Why did she stay with him, he thought curiously? Why had she attached herself to him? He couldn't help feeling that she had been sent to him. He thought of that first night in the jungle when he had cried out for help, and he pondered whether God had sent her. Or was it just coincidence?

Crack! Then shouting.

Toby and Gwen stared at each other in a new fear. A gunshot! No one in the tribe had had a gun. "Do you think … do you think it is … Tadeo?" Gwen whispered.

Toby hoped not. Tadeo had a deep desire to see them both dead. The tribe had probably just wanted them gone – one way or another. He peeped over the ferns at the sound. It was the same sound that chased him into the jungle on his arrival. He was not hopeful that it would be someone other than Tadeo.

A few minutes went by, and then he saw him, walking briskly along the path, looking over his shoulder. Tadeo. He had probably run into the tribe. They would have realized their spears were no match for his gun, and Toby imagined they had headed back to their village. Tadeo was muttering angrily to himself.

When Tadeo has passed them, Toby sat down, thinking. Would he come back? Toby guessed that he had probably been up and down the path once or twice already, looking for them. He would know it well, and would not have gotten lost. Toby glanced over at Gwen. Silent tears were rolling down her face.

"We're never going to get out of here, are we?" she asked him quietly. Truthfully, he was beginning to doubt it. He couldn't see how they could get passed Tadeo. He felt sure that Tadeo knew they were in there somewhere, and he didn't seem to be the kind of person to give up easily.

Toby wiped Gwen's tears with his thumbs and tried to reassure her. "Sure we will. We..." he was interrupted by several drops of rain, then, as before, the heavens opened. They crouched together under the ferns and surprisingly, only a little of the rain came through.

"I'm thirsty," whispered Gwen.

"That pool that we turned at was fed by a little stream as well as the waterfall, it was just off the other side of the path. When the rain stops, we'll find the stream and get a drink before we carry on," he said decidedly.

"What about Tadeo?" she asked worriedly.

"We'll just have to find a way past him," sighed Toby. Then he lied, "I'm sure we will be just fine. You'll see, this time tomorrow, you'll be in your bubble bath." Gwen smiled appreciatively.

"You never told me where you come from." Toby changed the subject. "You have an English accent."

"We used to live in England. Daddy decided to move us near New York two years ago. He said he could manage his business better there. We have a large estate in the country. The house is quite modern. Mommy said she did not want an old house that was cold and damp. I board at a private school during the week, and come home on the weekends. I could stay at the school, but I have a lovely black, Arabian mare, Ebony. I like to ride her on the weekends."

"Do you have many friends?" Toby asked.

"You have lots of friends when you are wealthy, Toby."

"Oh," Toby looked at her sad face thoughtfully. He couldn't tell if she was being cynical, or just upset about their predicament.

The rain stopped as suddenly as it started, and they crawled out of their hiding place and headed to the stream. They both bent down at the edge and, cupping their hands full of the cool liquid, drank thirstily.

Toby felt a sharp stab in his back and Gwen screamed. Turning around, he saw the two men who had caught them the day before, and his heart dropped. Gwen would not stop howling, and the smaller man growled at her, poking his spear at her cheek.

"Gwen," Toby tried to sound calm, talking loudly above the noise, "you need to stop. You are making them angry." She was close to hysterical.

"Please let us go! Someone help us, please!" She yelled at the top of her lungs and the men started poking harder with their spears.

Toby tried again. "Gwen, maybe if you are quiet they'll let us go. Maybe they just want to make sure we are leaving." He touched her arm comfortingly, and as her shouting subsided she took in great gulps of air, trying to control herself. He did not really believe for a minute that the men would let them go, but if it made her quiet, at least the men would not be so angry. Toby put his arm around Gwen and hugged her tightly.

"It'll be all right, Gwen, you'll see." Toby tried to believe his words. He'd almost convinced himself. Almost.

The men prodded Gwen and Toby with their spears and herded them slowly back to their village. Gwen continued gasping as she tried to hold back her screams. Toby thought she was going to hyperventilate. His own heart was beating so fast the blood was ringing in his ears. If these people were not sending them away, he could only see one reason for them to keep the teenagers. He closed his eyes, trying to shut out the pictures of horror that flashed in front of him. His imagination ran wild as he thought of all manner of ways that these people could kill them. None of them were quick.

They stumbled into the village, and their captors shoved the two to the ground at the chief's feet. Toby held on to Gwen tightly as they crouched on the ground. The chief began shouting out orders to various people, and they came running up to Gwen and Toby. Yanking the two apart, the women dragged Gwen in one direction and the men dragged Toby in another.

It was useless to protest, but he could hear Gwen screaming frantically again. Suddenly, her screeching was muffled. They had gagged her. Toby stood in the middle of a hut while the men stripped him of his clothes and threw them to the side. He stood in his boxers, wondering why they had left him that dignity. The taller man with the spear shoved a skin woven into a primitive kind of dress over his head and pulled his arms roughly through the sides. He then took some paint and smeared it over Toby's face. The finishing touch was a kind of crown woven of feathers that the man pressed down on Toby's head. A sticky brown liquid, not unlike molasses, lined the inside, stopping it from sliding off.

Toby coughed. He was still feeling achy and a headache began to grow and start pounding at his skull. No wonder, from all he had been through. He wondered how Gwen was.

When they had finished dressing him, they dragged Toby outside and into the middle of the village where two poles had been erected. Gwen came out shortly after, looking pretty much like he did, wearing a cloth tightly around her mouth.

Tears were running freely down her face as she walked jerkily towards him, the women pulling her along.

Putting Gwen and Toby back to back against the poles, the men tied their wrists together tightly and then to each post. Then they did the same with their ankles.

"Well," said Toby out loud, trying to calm Gwen. "At least there is no fire. They aren't burning us. Maybe they will just make us stand here and all day, humiliating us, before letting us go…" His words sounded stupid as he said them, but he was at a loss as to what was going to happen or what he could do. Toby heard some faint squeaking in the trees opposite him, and he saw Emmie sitting in one of the branches high up, curled tightly and watching him.

Maybe if they were tied up all night, Emmie would save them again. He could not think of any other way out. Except a miracle.

CHAPTER 16

SATURDAY 7th July – Doreen, Joe and Benito / Lucio's village

Doreen and Joe woke early the next morning, anxious to get going to find Toby and this girl. Benito curled up on his mattress, pretending to be asleep, hoping they would forget about him, cowardice overtaking him again. He would be quite happy to wait in the village for them. Surely they didn't need him to help. He was not very keen about putting himself in any more danger than he already had.

The two left Benito 'sleeping' and headed out to find Lucio and Rebeca, hoping they had come up with a good plan to get the teenagers back.

Rebeca met them outside, with the same breakfast she had give to Gwen and Toby a couple of days earlier, tortilla, beans, rice and avocado. Doreen and Joe were not that hungry, as they were anxious to get going, but Rebeca's insistence won out, and they sat down with her to eat, after she had gone into the hut with Benito's meal.

"He was still sleeping, but I just left it beside him," said Rebeca. They all ate slowly, and Joe tried to be patient, but finally could stand it no longer.

"So what is the plan?" he asked eagerly.

She sighed, and spoke quietly. "We have decided there is only one thing that we have that the chief of the Alejate desires greatly from us, and so I have finally convinced my father that I am right." She swallowed the last of her food and stood. "My father and I will go to the village, and you two can follow behind. You will not be needed." She looked at each of them. "You probably should wait here with Benito, but I believe you will not be persuaded to stay while we go."

Doreen and Joe shook their heads vehemently, and Doreen spoke up, "We must go with you, but you are right, it is probably best that you two are the only ones seen with your 'trade'. Joe and I will wait in the jungle, watching."

Rebeca strode off to her hut with determination, and Joe looked at Doreen. "I wonder what they have decided to trade?" he asked.

"I have an idea," said Doreen thoughtfully, "but I am hoping I am wrong."

⸻⸺◆⸺⸻

ALEJATE TRIBE – Toby and Gwen

As the sun began to rise higher in the sky, Toby and Gwen grew hotter and their legs grew more tired. Gwen had begun whimpering soon after they were tied to the poles together, and the pathetic sound continued off and on for most of the morning. Toby opened his mouth a couple of time to say something encouraging to Gwen but each time, his mind went blank and he closed his mouth again dejectedly.

The villagers just carried on about their daily business. Some were tending chickens while others took tools that looked like they might be harvesting something. While the two men that had captured them went off into the jungle with their spears, presumably to hunt some animal. Some young boys came up close to Toby and Gwen and called out something to them, then laughed. One punched another and they rolled about on the ground in quite a savage wrestle. Toby thought that maybe the parents or some adults would intervene, but an old woman walked by and chuckled as she saw the two boys scrapping, shouting what seemed to be some kind of encouragement to them.

Soon, he could feel Gwen pulling down slightly on their restrains, presumably because her legs were tired and could no longer support her body. Fresh weeping ensued and despite his own fear and desperation, Toby's heart went out to her, ashamed at himself for allowing themselves to be captured. He was supposed to be taking care of her. Okay, he hadn't asked to, but he was the male, after all. Though these days, it was all about equality. Still, Gwen seemed to *want* – no, *need* him to take care of her. In a month's time he would be eighteen – a man. And here he was, close to weeping along with the poor girl tied to him. He glanced up at the trees. Emmie was still up there watching them; though she had gotten herself a banana and was now munching away at it, while she watched them like some odd spectator at a horror movie.

Sweat began pouring off both of them and Toby thought perhaps his skin was beginning to bake and harden in the harsh sunlight. Gwen was more on the north side and was slightly shaded by Toby's taller frame. Toby had never known such oppressive heat. This must be what it felt like to be cooked alive in an oven on a low heat. His breathing was getting heavier and he could hear Gwen struggling to breath through her nose that had clogged up from her crying. Toby suddenly called out to a skinny young boy,

"Can't you take out her gag?!"

The boy looked at him puzzled and scooted off to a group of other boys that looked like they were playing some game with rocks. Of course, they probably did not understand English. Toby breathed out a deep sigh. So deep, that he struggled to draw his breath back in and set his heart rate racing in a panic attack. Though, he thought, perhaps dying from asphyxiation would be more desirable than what was ahead. The not knowing was the worst. Earlier, the chief had spoken to a few men, motioning, like he was organizing something. But they disappeared and nothing had happened.

Finally, when it must have been around noon, two women came out of one of the huts, each carrying a wooden cup. Toby's hopes grew.

"Look, Gwen, they are coming to give us a drink. Surely they would not give us a drink if they were going to do us any harm." He could feel Gwen put weight on her feet again and she made some soft moaning noises. When one of the women untied her gag, Gwen just opened her mouth, desperate for a drink. The other woman stood in front of Toby, and they each poured the warm sweet liquid in the teenagers' mouths. They each gulped thirstily and in their haste to consume the liquid, some of it ran down their chins. The woman in front of Toby smiled a sinister grin, and Toby's heart sank. Too late, he realized they had been drugged as her face started moving around in circles in front of him.

"Oh, Toby!" called out Gwen hoarsely, "My head is spinning. I ... don't ... feel ... well." He could hear the panic rising in her voice, but he could not make his lips form any intelligible words. Inconsolable wails rose in volume behind him as Gwen's hysteria grew and melded into a tornado around him.

A group of children held hands and encircled Toby and Gwen, dancing and chanting, slowly growing louder and faster as they danced and the tornado whirled, spinning Toby's thoughts and his breath frantically into a crescendo of movement until everything became a blur. A heavy damp cloud descended upon Toby with a crash, and then there was silence.

Toby blinked slowly several times, but each time he opened his eyes, all he could see was a thick, silent fog that was as oppressive as the earlier heat. He was drenched from the cold, damp fog and the silence was more absolute than he had ever experienced before. He was alone and could no longer feel the ties that bound his wrists and ankles. His body seemed to be absorbing the moisture around him like a sponge. A cold damp that seemed to penetrate into his bones, and he wondered if he was dead. A great blackness of fear consumed him and he cried out. He could feel the cry vibrate through his whole body and out his mouth, but there was no noise. Nothing. He was totally alone in a world of complete nothingness.

LUCIO'S tribe – Doreen and Joe

Doreen and Joe sat in silence on the ground, finishing the last of their breakfast absent-mindedly. Finally, Doreen spoke,

"Let's pray, Joe."

"I have been," he answered, but looked down at her extended hands, and took hold of them. They held hands tightly as they prayed for safety and help.

Benito came out of the hut just then and started talking as he walked towards them, then went silent as he saw their heads bowed, voices lowered. He wondered about this praying business. Did God actually hear them? And if He did, did He care? How powerful *was* God, anyway? Could He really save Toby and Gwen? He had heard them talking about the Alejate; Benito knew about that tribe. They sacrificed people that they captured to their gods. Was Doreen and Joe's God stronger than the Alejate gods?

Benito sat down beside them and began quietly eating his breakfast. He was quite hungry and he always enjoyed the food when he came to Nicaragua. There was not as much variety as back in England, but somehow, everything tasted so much better. Maybe because it was all so fresh.

Doreen let go of Joe's hands as they finished praying. She turned to Benito. "You must stay here, Benito," she spoke firmly, as though she had to persuade him. Benito stifled the relieved grin welling up inside him and tried to look disappointed. "There is no need for you to go with us." She looked at Joe before adding, "There probably isn't anything we can do, either, but Joe and I must accompany Rebeca and her father just in case there is some way – *any* way, we can help." Benito nodded, concentrating on shovelling down his food. He could have done with twice as much.

Just then, Rebeca came out of her hut. Joe was shocked at the transformation. She had on a plain white blouse, with a gathered peasant neckline, and a long, full brightly coloured skirt. A red and gold shawl hung loosely across her shoulders. Thin gold ribbons wound their way through her shiny black hair. Gold and red paint around her eyes made them look wide and a deep red covered her full lips. Gold earrings and bangles clinked softly as she padded softly down the steps in her leather sandals. She wore a determined look as she walked purposefully towards them.

Joe started to speak, but was interrupted by the appearance of Lucio from their hut, dressed elaborately in brightly coloured clothes decorated with an amazing collection of feathers. Rebeca's grandmother came out behind him, dressed as she had been the previous day. They both walked over to Rebeca, and her grandmother hugged her firmly, talking animatedly in their own language. She held Rebeca's face with both of her hands, and kissed both her cheeks, before turning and walking away.

"What is going on? Why are you dressed like that?" asked Joe he looked at Lucio and then Rebeca. Lucio said a few short words, and Rebeca translated.

"It is time to go, and offer the bride," she said simply, and smiled bravely.

Joe stood open mouthed, horrified at the revelation, and Doreen sighed deeply. "We can't let you do this," Doreen said sensibly. There must be another way. We are just trading a life for ..."

Joe interrupted, grabbing Rebeca by the shoulders. "No! You can't! You can't sacrifice yourself. We'll fight them! We'll take spears and guns and fight them!"

Rebeca gently squeezed Joe's hands, and pulled them from her shoulders. They stood facing each other, both with feet firmly planted in a determined stance, holding hands while several moments passed.

"Their chief has asked several times that I be married to his son, Mundo. His son has wanted me since he was a boy." She smiled, then touched Joe's cheek with her fingers. "It is still our custom sometimes, to marry this way. We are not like England where it is all romantic and people marry because they are in love."

"But ..." Joe started.

"It is all right, Joe. Maybe it is God's plan for me to be an influence for Him in this tribe. Mundo will one day be chief in his father's place, and I will have much authority along side him. It will also benefit my father and our tribe. There is often trouble between the two tribes, and with me as Mundo's wife, there should finally be reconciliation between us."

"But it isn't what you want, sweetheart," said Doreen, "We really appreciate your amazing sacrifice, but you can't."

"I have given it much thought, Doreen, and I am a very determined person." She turned to her father and said something to him. He nodded, and smiled lovingly at his only daughter. "You will not change my mind."

Benito sat in stunned silence, as he marvelled at Rebeca. What a girl! It made him hate his own weakness even more, and he hung his head in shame as the four said goodbye to him and walked towards the jungle path to trade Rebeca for Toby and Gwen.

Lucio led the way through the narrow path with Rebeca right behind him, and Doreen and Joe taking up the rear. No one said anything as they walked at a steady pace. Birds squawked and tweeted and peeped. Monkeys chattered and shouted. Insects buzzed and chirped. They all blended into a chorus as the four walked along, hoping against hope, and praying too, that Toby and Gwen were still alive.

Rebeca felt oddly calm after her fitful sleep last night. The idea had come to her in the early hours of the night and she had woken her father to tell him. It wasn't a new idea. Mundo's father had been a couple of times recently to speak to her father. He was of age now, and wanted a wife. Mundo and she had first met years ago, when they were ten. Rebeca had been fishing at a river several miles away with girls from their village, when Mundo and a couple of boys had come along with spears in their hands, holding up a small deer proudly. Although their languages were different, there were some similarities, and when Mundo had looked at her and said a few words, she understood enough to know he was saying that she would join the Alejate tribe and be his wife. She had had several fish beside her, and Mundo thought it would be good to have a fine fisher-woman as his bride.

Over the years, she had seen him a couple of times when she went out fishing, and each time, he declared his intentions to her. Rebeca had laughed at him. She had always had other ideas. Ideas of getting a good education. Perhaps becoming a teacher, or even travelling to her mother's homeland and teaching there. Her mother used to tell her wonderful stories about where she came from. She told Rebeca about electricity and indoor plumbing – Rebeca would never again have to haul water. Televisions and trains and ice cream. She would like to taste ice cream … and she would like to go ice skating. So many things in the world to try.

But this morning she had changed her mind. It really was the only way to rescue Toby and Gwen and, like she had said, maybe God did have a plan for her to be an influence with the Alejates. And there would be no more fighting with her own tribe. Maybe this was the future God had planned for her. And once she had made up her mind, she felt completely at peace, confident that it was the right decision.

CHAPTER 17

After an hour walking in silence, Lucio stopped and said something to Rebeca. She turned to Doreen and Joe.

"You two must wait here. The Alejate are just ahead to the left. You must be patient, as it may take some time. There will be some negotiation between my father and Mundo's father. My father will come back this way once he has Toby and Gwen." Without another word, she turned and headed with her father towards her fate.

Joe and Doreen stood there for a moment. When Rebeca and Lucio were out of sight, Joe turned to Doreen. "We have to get closer so we can see. I can't just stay here and wait without knowing what is going on." Doreen nodded her head. "I am sure we can hide in some bushes and watch without being found."

So the two of them followed in the direction that Lucio and Rebeca had taken, and when they could see a clearing in the distance, they carefully made their way into some deep bushes and ferns and carefully crept closer until they could get a good view of the village and see what was happening. The noises of the jungle were loud, and they were confident of being able to get close without being seen or heard.

Finally, they came to the edge of the clearing and hid behind some amazingly large ferns. It was a perfect vantage point to see the majority of the village. Doreen and Joe could see Lucio and Rebeca standing beside the first hut. A man with a spear was stopping them from going further, while they waited for the chief and Mundo.

Doreen gasped as her eyes landed on Toby and Gwen tied in the middle of the huts. Their skin was red from the harsh sun and their bodies glistened from the perspiration that covered them. They stood slumped, held up only by their ties, their heads flopped forward, occasionally lolling from side to side. Joe's heart caught in his throat and he covered Doreen's mouth firmly with his hand, masking the noise she made.

"We must be quiet, Aunty Doreen," he whispered, trying to remain calm himself, but anger at the tribe slowly seeping through his whole body.

"But look at them, Joe! Oh, look at them, they are passed out from the heat!" Just then, Gwen lifted her head, and her eyes rolled around in her drug induced stupor, and Doreen gasped again.

Suddenly, their attention was drawn back to Lucio and Rebeca, as what looked like the chief and his son walked towards them. Mundo was as tall as his father, but slimmer. He wore a silly grin on his face, and the chief looked pleased as well when they saw Rebeca. Lucio and the chief exchanged words, while Mundo reached for Rebeca's hands. She lowered her head and bowed slightly in a submissive manner.

Many words passed between them, and Doreen and Joe looked on hopefully. But when Lucio motioned to Toby and Gwen, the chief got annoyed and shook his head. The discussion grew in animation and Joe and Doreen began to get worried.

The chief motioned for Lucio and Rebeca to join them at the far edge of the huts under the shade of a large tree, and the four of them sat down. The chief shouted at someone and after a few moments, was brought a couple of pipes that had smoke coming from them. The two chiefs sat talking, smoking the pipes, while Rebeca and Mundo sat silently, waiting for them to come to some kind of decision.

Doreen and Joe grew impatient as they watched and waited. How long would it take before something happened? Would they be able to take Toby home with them? And get that poor girl back to her family?

Stretching a leg to the side, Doreen groaned quietly. "Oh, my legs are aching in this position." She stretched the other one out. "I am too old to be crouched in a jungle," she admitted.

Despite the situation, Joe smiled. "Old, you are not, Aunty Doreen," then added, "My legs are aching in this position as well. Why don't you go back there in the jungle a bit, and stretch out while I keep watch. Then we can swap. If someone starts heading our way, we can warn each other."

Doreen reluctantly agreed to leave their post, feeling hopeless and distressed at the sight of Toby tied to the poles. That poor girl, her parents must be worried sick.

She crept several metres back into the jungle until she came to a space where she could stretch her arms and legs and walk around in a small circle. She paced back and forth for a few moments, stretching all her limbs as she did so.

Soon, Doreen was drawn back to Joe, anxious to see if there had been any agreement. Joe sighed deeply. "They just look like they are getting stoned," he said in disgust. Every time he looked at his brother, the anger inside him grew. Everything within him wanted to jump out with a stick and beat each one of these people senseless. It was all he could do stay where he was.

Just then, Rebeca stood up, stretched out her arms and legs, and walked casually towards Toby and Gwen. The chief shouted something at her, and Lucio calmed him down with reassuring sounding words, motioning the chief to take another puff, then they both broke out in laughter. Mundo watched suspiciously, but did not move.

Rebeca reached Gwen and stroked her face. She said something to some children standing by, and motioned at them. Two of them ran off and quickly came back with a small bucket of water and a cloth. Rebeca took the cloth and dipped it in the cool water, using it to gently bath Gwen's hot head and neck. She then rubbed her arms and legs. When no one stopped her, she moved around and did the same to Toby. Neither of them flinched.

Mundo stared on in admiration of her strong character. He could not decide if that was a good characteristic in a wife. But then, he thought, she had come in quiet submission. No, Mundo felt certain he could keep her in her place. She would fill their dishes with much fish, as well. He laughed at his private joke, but the two chiefs were too engrossed in their conversation and pipes to take any notice of him.

Rebeca kept wiping the wet cloth over Toby and Gwen until all the water in the bucket was gone. She touched their skin and was pleased to find they were both much cooler.

Suddenly, Toby's eyes opened wide and he grabbed Rebeca's arm. Startled, she stepped back and tripped on the bucket, falling to the ground. Young boys standing by burst out laughing and jumped on her. Mundo started to get up, but Rebeca picked herself up and spoke firmly to the boys, shooing them away fiercely. Mundo smiled. He liked this woman. When he was chief, he could leave her in charge of the whole village and they would all do as they were told. Now, if only his father would agree.

Rebeca looked back at Toby, but his head had dropped back down again. She shook her head. They had been given a lot of drug. Reluctantly, she left the two teenagers and went back to sit with the two chiefs and Mundo.

Two hours later, Rebeca and her father stood, and Doreen and Joe watched hopefully. Their hopes were dashed when they headed to the entrance of the village. Joe and Doreen crept back to where Lucio and Rebeca had left them, waiting for their return.

As they came into view, Joe grabbed Doreen's arm, "Look!"

Two men with spears followed the chief and his daughter. When the men saw Joe and his aunt, they shouted at them and they froze. Rebeca wore a sad expression and Lucio just wore a vacant look from smoking the pipe for so long.

"We are being escorted back to our village." Explained Rebeca quietly. "Do not speak until we get there, or you will make them angry."

⸺⸺◆⸺⸺

At the opposite side of the village, evil blue eyes peered through the bushes at the teenagers tied to the posts. Tadeo smiled vindictively: They were getting what they deserved. This would solve his problem without him lifting a finger. A perfect solution!

A faint squeaking in a tree nearby drew his attention. It was that little monkey. She was sticking to the boy like she belonged to him. Smart little thing. Very smart. She could get Tadeo a lot of money from the right person. He knew the right people. A nice little bonus for his troubles, if he could catch her. He would make a trap. Yes, he deserved a bonus.

⸺⸺◆⸺⸺

Hesitantly, Doreen and her nephew turned around and reluctantly allowed themselves to be herded back to Lucio and Rebeca's home.

The pace was quick on the return, and Doreen grew quite tired from walking the rough ground and from all the stress, and she began to stumble. Joe held her arm and the two of them walked side by side in silence, gathering strength from each other's presence.

Finally, the path through the jungle opened up into the clearing, and the huts came into view. As they walked out, the two men stood by the path like sentinels with their spears. Lucio walked to their hut and slowly climbed the stairs wavering from side to side, while Rebeca walked over to her grandmother who was sitting in the middle by the fire cooking some fish that others had caught. She spoke to her in their own tongue, and they hugged each other, before Rebeca turned and motioned for Doreen and Joe to sit with them and eat while she explained to them what had been decided. Benito had been lying down in the hut to escape the heat of the sun, but came out and joined them when he heard their voices. He was surprised to see Rebeca was with them.

"What happened?" he queried.

Rebeca pursed her lips as she thought of the best way to explain things, without worrying Toby's family needlessly.

"Xochilt, the chief, wanted us to come back tomorrow," she began.

Everyone looked at her as she hesitated, then continued, choosing her words carefully. "The Alejate have been plagued with Grisi Siknis. Many young folk have been getting it."

Three questioning faces stared at her.

"It is like a spirit possession. They become crazy and very strong. If they can be caught and tied down, sometimes the sukia – the healing man – can give them potions and say … incantations, calling on their gods for healing."

The three looked doubtfully at her. She understood their scepticism, but she had seen it before. It had happened a couple of times in their own village. As a Christian, she did not understand it, but she felt protected from it so she was not afraid.

"Gwen's hair was burned into an ash, then put into a potion that appeared to heal one of their girls." She swallowed before she explained further. "The chief believes that the gods would be appeased and all Grisi Siknis would go away, if they sacrificed Gwen to them. Toby would be an extra sacrifice for 'good luck', as you westerners say."

Doreen covered her mouth in horror and she began breathing heavily. Joe put his arm around her and held her tightly.

"So why will you go back tomorrow?" Joe's heart pounded against his chest in terror for his brother, but he needed to know all the facts.

"Because, the sacrifice is not always accepted."

"What do you mean?" asked Joe.

"The Alejate tie up their sacrifice and put them out on ledge by a steep cliff just past their village. They leave them there over night. If they are still there in the morning, the gods have rejected the sacrifice and the Alejate let the people go. They are no good to them."

"Well," said Joe, "There are no 'gods', so the sacrifices must always surely be there the next morning."

Rebeca did not really want to say anymore, as Doreen looked like she was going to pass out and Joe looked like he was close to slaughtering the whole village himself, but she decided she needed to tell the truth.

"The sacrifice is covered completely in blood before it is left. There are wild animals in the jungle that are big enough to drag a human away. The tribe are so superstitious, this does not occur to them. They just believe the 'gods' took them."

"No!" panicked Doreen. She had been so confident they would get Toby back. This was a terrible nightmare. Surely she would wake up any minute. What was God doing??! He was just standing by while her poor nephew was being mistreated, drugged and possibly fed to animals. Her breathing came even faster, and she was close to hyperventilating. Joe held his arm around her tightly.

"Come on, Aunty Doreen, you need to calm down. You are no good to Toby if you have a meltdown." His calm voice belied his own feelings. Feelings of growing rage. Feelings of wanting to take things into his own hands. His faith in God was beginning to waver.

"We must pray that God will protect them, and keep them safe until tomorrow," spoke Rebeca determinedly.

"But," began Joe, "if they just let the people go if the 'gods' don't take them, won't they just let Toby and Gwen go tomorrow?"

"My father and I have offered myself in marriage. They would not take kindly to my changing my mind and we would not go against our offer. That is not acceptable. We will go back with those men," she motioned to the two standing guard, "at first light."

The sun had set and they gathered closer to the fire as Rebeca's grandmother motioned to them to come for some food. The fish was ready. Joe and Doreen were devoid of appetite, but Rebeca encouraged them to eat to keep up their strength. Benito, of course, had no such hesitation and tucked eagerly into the offered food.

———◆———

ALEJATE TRIBE – SATURDAY 7th July / Toby and Gwen

Time stood still while Toby was in the damp cloud. He did not know how long he was there. He started feeling wetter and wetter. Suddenly, he saw a dark figure in front of him with a black cloth, but something prevented him from running, some unknown force was holding him there. The black cloth had a cold black liquid dripping from it and the figure was wiping him with it. He got colder and colder and the liquid was making his skin turn black. For a brief moment, he felt strength in his left arm and grabbed the figure, who looked up at him. A flash of Rebeca's face appeared, and then it was gone, and so was the black figure. He could see the black liquid dripping off of him, and he was alone again in this empty place. His heart was pounding heavily against his chest, desperate to wake up, to escape this nothingness.

Ever so slowly, the cloud began to fade, and Toby began to feel warmer. Tingling entered other parts of his body and he could faintly hear the noise of the village, as though they were far away. The cloud finally gave way to darkness, lit by an orange glow that waved its arms back and forth randomly to a song that had no voice.

Toby blinked. A fire was lit in the middle and the whole tribe was gathered, eating their meal and talking animatedly. His body ached from the position he had been in all day, but he welcomed the feeling after the nothingness that he had woken up from. It meant he was alive. Behind him, Gwen began to whine like a scared and injured puppy.

"Gwen," he said with much effort. "Gwen, are you all right?" He wondered if she had experienced the same thing as him.

"I have a terrible headache," she spoke hoarsely. "I had a terrible nightmare ... with lots of dark figures ... but it is all so ... I can't remember any of it ... I think I am glad."

Toby was glad, too. He wouldn't wish his experience on his worst enemy. His head was pounding and his throat was sore. It took great effort to talk, but he wanted to encourage her.

"It looks like they have forgotten all about us. They will probably go to bed soon and then hopefully Emmie will come down and rescue us like before. This time we will make it to the town."

"Emmie?" she questioned feebly.

He nodded, though Gwen could not see him.

"Ya, she has been up in that tree across from me all day, watching. I bet as soon as everyone is tucked up asleep, she will come down and bite our ropes again." He spoke hopefully, but he picked up the anticipation that was permeating the group, and a sick feeling in the pit of his stomach began to grow.

Just then, the chief glanced over at them and saw they were waking up. He motioned to the two women who had given Toby and Gwen the drugged drink earlier, and they got up and went inside a hut. Toby wished he and Gwen had pretended they were still out of it. A few minutes later, they came out, each with a cup and instinctively, Toby closed his mouth. Gwen began sobbing,

"No!" she called out weakly, "No more!" But as she opened her mouth to shout, the woman poured the liquid down her throat. Toby could hear Gwen gagging as the woman poured the entire cup in and shut her mouth tightly with her hands. The woman in front of Toby would not be put off by his tightly closed lips, and she pried them open with strong fingers and sharp nails. She held Toby's nose as he gagged down the liquid. It tasted different to the last one and Toby was not sure if that was good or not. He was about to find out.

A jug was passed around the tribe and everyone took a drink, even the children. They laughed as they drank and then one by one they all stood and started singing and dancing around the fire, and around Toby and Gwen.

Everything started spinning faster and faster, and the music seemed to grow louder. The members of the tribe began painting each other with brightly coloured paints and continued to laugh and dance and sing as they did so.

A cold wind that seemed to have an essence of life, whipped its way through the village and around the people. They reached out their hands as though they could touch it. The wind churned up the dust and the fire cracked loudly as it danced along with the Alejate people. They all had their hands in the air, moving and swaying in the wind. They looked like they were seeing something in the air. Toby looked up.

For a moment, he saw nothing. Then, one by one, they came into sight. Horrible flying creatures. Razor sharp teeth and huge black eyes on pale pitted faces. Long scraggly hair flew behind them as they dove and danced in the air around the fire. Long tongues slithered out like snakes as they flew by Toby and Gwen and they laughed a hideous laugh as they scraped Toby's face with their long, pointed claws. They each had three black tails that seemed to dance behind them like they had a life of their own. Toby closed his eyes as each one came by and ducked each time they did. He wondered if Gwen was seeing the same thing.

As if in answer, a piercing shriek reverberated through his back as Gwen collapsed into full blown hysteria. This time though, the villagers did not seem upset. In fact, they screamed along with her and their laughter mimicked Gwen's hysteria as they danced faster and faster, working themselves into a frenzy.

The chief nodded to a man on his right, and he danced over to Toby and Gwen with a knife.

"Please God make it quick," thought Toby as the man twirled and jumped towards him, singing louder than the others. Then Toby realized the man sounded louder because the others had stopped singing. They had begun chanting in a haunting whisper and were now standing, watching as the man came closer. Toby closed his eyes, not wanting to see when the knife was near. Then, in four swift swipes, his ankles and wrists were free!

Just as Toby was rejoicing, he and Gwen collapsed on the ground. Neither of them could stand; in fact, all their muscles felt incredibly weak. Three men came towards them, and two of them lifted Gwen above their heads. The other one joined the man with the knife and picked up Toby. The whole tribe shouted as the men danced back towards the fire and the flying creatures swooped lower and faster.

They all trotted three times around the fire, then headed off down a narrow path. The men carrying Toby and Gwen above their heads, followed the chief, who led the way. The chanting continued as the whole village walked along briskly.

They must have walked for fifteen minutes, and Toby wished he could cover his ears. Every time Gwen let out a wail, the whole group wailed with her, and then they laughed along with the flying things that flitted their way through the dense vegetation, every now and then, skimming Toby's face lightly with their bat like wings or their alarming claws.

The chanting changed rhythm, and the crowd gathered into a semicircle around Toby and Gwen as they were dropped heavily on a large stone slab. Gwen and Toby tried to brace themselves for the fall, but found the weakness had grown to paralysis. They could not move – anything. Toby tried to speak to Gwen to see if she was okay, but not even his voice worked.

They lay helpless on the slab, back to back, two sprawling bodies unable to move. It was too dark to see, but Toby sensed there was some kind of drop on the other side. He did not want to think about how far down it was.

The chief held a flaming torch, and waved it high in the night sky, toward the full moon, and they all dropped to their knees as someone stepped forward with a large jug and poured a warm thick liquid all over Gwen and Toby, until Toby felt like he was swimming in it. He did not want to think about what it was, and trying to close his eyes and mouth tightly, but he could feel some if it running in his nostrils, and he coughed.

A great shout rose up and each of them began to make a strange whistling, gurgling sound, waving their hands in the air wildly. Then, as though one being, they all fell on their knees, slapping their hands on the ground – and there was silence. Even the creatures, though Toby could feel the swishing as they flew past back and forth, no longer made a sound.

Several moments later, Toby squinted open his sticky eyes: they were the only thing that functioned. The people were gone.

He was about to breathe a sigh of relief, when he saw the creatures, still flying back and forth. There were hundreds of them now, like a swarm of locusts waiting to devour a field of wheat. Except they were not locusts, and there was no wheat. Just Gwen and him.

Toby suddenly realized that though the night was heavy with the creatures, they no longer came close to them. They had begun making noises again, but this time it was like angry mob whispering loudly as they darted about. Toby felt a warmth by his feet and he looked towards them. A glowing figure stood with hands outstretched. It looked like the same figure he had seen on his drug-induced trip to the moon. Toby could not distinguish a face. And then it was gone. Along with the creatures. Slowly, the jungle came alive with the night sounds, and Toby wondered if the 'regular' animals had been frightened into silence by the flying beasts. Little lights flitted back and forth. Fireflies. Toby watched as they seemed to dance happily in the darkness like disco lights. A much more pleasurable dance than the frantic movements of the village and the vile flying things. He wondered when the people would be back.

Just then, some distant high pitched barking began, and Toby wondered if the dogs in the village had been disturbed by something. But then, terror filled him as he realized the sound was not dogs, but coyotes. And they were coming closer. They were probably drawn by the tacky stuff that had been poured on him and Gwen.

If only he could move his arms, he could at least try to defend himself. A picture flashed in his mind of being chewed apart by coyotes while he and Gwen lay conscious but frozen on the ground, and Toby felt sickness rise up through his throat and out his mouth, pooling out onto the slab.

The barking stopped, and Toby hoped they had found something else for their dinner. His hopes were dashed as he heard a sniffing sound by his feet. Then more sniffing, all around him and Gwen as the rest of the pack arrived. They started to growl as they each fought for position and started licking up the sticky substance that had been poured on the teenagers. Toby prayed that Gwen had passed out, and then he prayed that he would pass out. He closed his eyes so he would not see what was happening, and he prayed for a rescue.

At once, there was an explosion of noise from the trees surrounding them. Shrieks and screams and loud squeaks awakened the night and Toby looked up as small figures swung low above him, tossing down tiny objects of some kind at the coyotes. They barked and growled up at the monkeys but slowly, one by one, they slunk off into the jungle to find an easier meal.

Toby's eyes had adjusted to the dark, and he could see a small monkey huddling a few feet from him, tucked away under a bush. Other monkeys were bouncing around, some still squeaking and others chattering, like they were having a conversation with the monkey under the bush. It must be

Emmie — had she been there all the time? Had she been in danger from the coyotes as well? Her troop must have come to rescue her and inadvertently rescued Gwen and Toby in the process. Wow! He had no idea that monkeys could defend themselves against a pack of coyotes. Lucky for him and Gwen. Or *was* it luck? Rebeca did not seem to think there was any such thing. Did God send the monkeys? Did He protect them from those ugly flying creatures that the Alejate had somehow conjured up? He *was* drugged. Maybe he had imagined everything. Though this time, the drug did not seem to affect his mind, only his body. But then, how did he know that this was not all just a dreadful nightmare?

Toby sighed with immense relief, and could feel Gwen's heavy breathing against his back. She must have been awake through it all — she would have been as terrified as he had been. He really had failed her. His relief turned into deep despondency as he wondered if he would ever manage to get the two of them back to civilization.

A thought struck him. He had seen Rebeca when he was in the wet cloud — had she actually been there? If so, she knew where they were. Perhaps she was organizing a rescue party. But then ... Toby's thoughts drifted into a deep dark sleep as the adrenaline drained from his body, joining the sticky mess that lay on the stone beneath him.

CHAPTER 18

SUNDAY 8th July – Lucio's tribe

Doreen and Joe had barely slept the night before, and at first ray of sun, were up and dressed. Joe looked down scornfully at Benito, softly snoring on his bed. He turned to Doreen. "I find it very difficult not to despise him, Aunty Doreen."

Doreen stepped towards her nephew and gave him a tight squeeze, and they stood silently hugging each other for comfort for a moment before she answered. "He has had a very rough life, sweetheart, just remember that. Who knows how you would have turned out if you had lived in his shoes?"

Joe pursed his lips and shook his head. He said determinedly, "I would have been tougher than him."

Doreen stepped back and held him by the shoulders, looking up at him thoughtfully. "I worry about you, Joe."

Joe was taken aback. "What do you mean, worried about *me*? It's Toby you need to be worried about."

"I worry about your pride, Joe. If you don't let it go, it will cause you grief. You remember what the Bible says, 'Pride comes before destruction and an arrogant spirit before a fall.' Have compassion on Benito, like God has had compassion on you and your weaknesses."

Joe smirked, "Aunt Doreen, my weaknesses are nowhere near as bad as that little worm lying there." And with that he turned abruptly away from Doreen and strutted out the doorway and down the stairs.

Doreen stood there for a moment thinking, and praying, that Joe did not really believe what he had just said. A few moments later, they were all gathered by the fire, eating their breakfast. Rebeca was dressed exactly as she had the previous day, and was sat on the steps of her hut eating her breakfast, wanting to be alone in her thoughts for a moment.

While Joe looked at her as he began eating, he felt his admiration for her grow even stronger than it had the day before, and a sad pang knocked against his chest. He looked down at his food. He could not eat anything else. In a few hours, they would find out if they had lost Toby or would lose Rebeca. It was beyond comprehension. What was God doing? For as long as he could remember, he had had a knowledge of God's presence. A strong faith that nothing had deterred. Now, scepticism was creeping through him like the first frost of autumn.

Benito interrupted his thoughts as he burst out the door and trotted down the steps with a smile on his face. He looked at Joe and the smile disappeared. A deep desire to jump Benito and pummel him senseless raged through Joe, and it was all he could do to sit still. He scowled angrily at Benito, who decided to sit as far away as possible, feeling this grace thing might just disappear into oblivion at any minute.

A few minutes later, Rebeca put down her plate and stood up.

"Es tiempo de irse," her father spoke, and Joe glanced over at the shadow of their hut. He had not seen the chief, and wondered how long he had been standing there. As much as it was their tradition, Joe wondered if Rebeca's father, too, had a heart that was breaking.

"It is time to go," translated Rebeca.

Silently, the group headed off towards the path. Amazingly, the two men with spears were still standing guard. As they reached them, the men turned around and led the way into the jungle.

⟫●⟪

SUNDAY 8th July – Toby and Gwen

Toby started to cry as the water splashed in his nose and mouth making him cough as he floundered in the deep pool. The bottom seemed miles away and the noise of the other children which magnified tenfold in the large building, only panicked him more. He couldn't do it. His body would not cooperate as his mind emptied of everything but the water that surrounded him, pulling him down. He was going to drown! His head went under the surface as his thrashing became more wild and any semblance of swimming from his limbs disappeared. But just when he thought he was going to sink to the bottom, he heard his mother's calm, encouraging voice.

"Toby! Look at me, sweetheart. Calm down. You can do it." He looked up and saw her smiling face and outstretched arms. She was miles away …

Toby could hear a voice cry out. Was it his own voice? "Moooommmmyyyy!!"

"Toby, remember what I showed you."

Toby tried desperately to focus on her smiling face.

"Toby, swim to me, darling." Her soothing voice placated his panic and, ever so slowly, his thrashing became more orderly and he began to move his arms and legs in the way she had shown him. There was still lots of splashing, and some water was still getting in his face, but he was moving forward. He concentrated on his mom's face and her encouraging voice as every muscle in his arms and legs strained to reach her.

"Swim to mommy, Toby, swim to mommy. Come on Toby."

"You're doing it, honey! Keep going."

As his strokes became more methodical, he gritted his teeth and swam faster.

"Come on Toby! You are nearly here! Come on Toby. Come on Toby. Toby. Toby. Bark Bark Bark."

A strange noise was invading his unconsciousness, drawing him out like the gentle outstretched arms of his mom. Suddenly, Toby opened his eyes, and saw Emmie, sitting there, a few feet away from him. She looked like she was desperate to snuggle him, but would not go near the sticky mess. Toby strained to keep his eyes open and saw in the pre-dawn light that the sticky mess was a dark red. Blood? That would make sense. Although he could feel his body now, he could not make anything move. Finally, he managed to wiggle his fingers. Then his toes.

"Gwen," he could barely hear his own voice. Breathing deeply, he tried again, "Gwen," a whisper this time. Putting in all the energy he could muster, he tried a third time, "Gwen!" and startled at the sound of his voice.

He heard a faint whine behind him. Then, "Toby."

He sighed with relief. Good. Then, soft weeping, and he felt her body gently shaking with her tears.

"It's all right, Gwen," he mustered, "We are okay." He spoke in a near normal voice now, but his limbs were still uncooperative. He kept on wiggling his fingers and toes and soon found his feet and hands moving. Encouraged, he spoke to Gwen, "Gwen, wiggle your toes and fingers as much as you can. The more you wiggle, the faster you will be able to move the rest of your body."

The weeping stopped but Gwen continued to sniffle as she concentrated on wiggling, and shortly, she let out a weak cry,

"I can move my hands and feet, Toby!"

By this time, Toby's arms and legs were moving; slowly, but they were moving. With great effort, he turned over to face Gwen and impulsively reached his arm around her in a gentle hug. She snuggled into his embrace and they lay there, their faces inches apart. Tenderly, he tried to brush the blood off of her cheek, but it had dried on. He left his hand lying gently on her face, the back of his fingers resting on her soft skin as he looked at her. She smiled faintly and Toby's heart beat a little faster.

How could she still be so beautiful? Her dark, full lips were drawing him toward her.

He had only kissed a girl once before. It was his next door neighbour and friend, Katy Thompson. He was twelve at the time, and his best friend, Adam had told Toby that he would only be able to tell if he liked a girl if he kissed her. Katy and he were just leaning over the fence talking, and he kissed her impulsively. Immediately, Toby regretted his action, fearing for their friendship.

After a few awkward moments staring at each other, they burst out laughing, and Toby had sighed with relief. They were still friends. And in that moment they both knew that was all they would be. But that was okay, and they continued to be good friends all the way through high school.

Gwen's warm breath drew him back to the present, lying there, her emerald eyes drawing him closer. Toby's heart began pounding loudly and he wondered if Gwen could hear, as he bent forward and touched his lips to hers. They were incredibly soft and he seemed to melt into them. When she responded eagerly, electricity shot through him and he felt the feeling return in the rest of his body as the blood raced through him. He had never felt anything like this before. He could barely breath.

"Screech! Screech! Screech!"

Emmie's frantic calls pierced their embrace and Toby turned to see what was the matter. He heard Gwen "huff" as he did. She grabbed his arm and pulled him back towards her.

"Kiss me again!" she smiled demurely, and Toby pressed his lips against hers again, but with less energy, his thoughts now distracted by the little monkey.

"Oh Toby! Kiss me like the first time." He tilted his head and chuckled.

"I think Emmie is telling us we need to go." Toby said, getting to his feet and trying to pull off all the feathers stuck to his head. He was a little wobbly, but he felt the strength returning with every passing minute. He held out his hand to Gwen, and she reluctantly took it, her ruby lips now pouting in disappointment.

"Stupid animal!" she complained sharply and immediately, Toby became annoyed. It was odd how emotions could change so quickly.

"She saved our lives last night, you know." He retorted.

"How?"

"Well, not her directly, but she was hiding under that bush, and when the coyotes came ..."

"Coyotes?!" Gwen's eyes grew wide with fear. Evidently she had not been awake when the coyotes had come.

Toby was unsure whether to continue, and spare Gwen the upset, but he wanted to defend Emmie so stubbornly, he carried on.

"Yes, coyotes came and they were going to ... anyway, when they came, Emmie was hiding under the bush and her family came to defend her." He paused, mulling it over. "I think they thought the coyotes were after her. They threw things at the coyotes, brave little things, and the coyotes went away." Toby paused, his thoughts churning. If the troop had come to save Emmie, they must be near where he first met Emmie. If he could get there, perhaps he could find his way back to Rebeca's tribe and hopefully, finally, a way home.

Emmie was still jumping up and down, but she would not come near them.

"We need to wash off," said Toby, "But first, we need to go." The sun had risen above the horizon and bright rays had just reached their ledge. Toby looked around and bit his lip. "We are going to have to try and go down." He motioned towards the steep edge, and Gwen frowned.

"Why *that* way?" she asked worriedly.

"Because the only other way is the path back towards where we came from, and I don't think either of us want to go back *there*." He paused, half smiling, "Besides, it isn't as bad as it looks, there are lots of bushes to grab hold of as we go down. Come on." He pulled Gwen's hand gently, and reluctantly she followed. Emmie was still screeching, but softer now and, jumping into a tree, she swung expertly behind the teenagers struggling down the steep incline, grabbing onto branches and vines to stop themselves from falling.

Gwen started slipping and she reached out to grab a branch, but missed and let out a scream. Floundering forward, she began rolling through the thick undergrowth, crying out in agony at each bounce.

"Toby! " Toby was helpless as she tumbled to the bottom, but he hurried along as fast as he could, stumbling and nearly falling also. He slowed a little, torn between being desperate to reach Gwen and realizing he wouldn't be any use to her if he fell and hurt himself.

"Gwen!" he cried as she hit the bottom hard and lay motionless, face to the ground, underneath a large fern. Toby increased his speed again, stumbling and tripping the rest of the way down, crashing through the bushes, finally reaching her side.

"Gwen!" he called out again, as he knelt beside her and grabbed her shoulders gently to turn her over, holding her on his lap. Immediately he regretted his actions. What if she had a back injury? He exhaled deeply. There would be little chance of him getting help for her.

Gwen's head rested in his arms, and he unsuccessfully tried to brush the soil off of her face that had now mixed with the dried blood. He leaned down and hugged her tightly, rocking back and forth. "Oh, Gwen."

This time, a soft moaning answered him. Loosening his grip he looked down at her, her green eyes slowly opening into a slightly dazed stare. Toby stroked her face gently and kissed her forehead, repeating her name over and over. She smiled faintly at his affections, then finally spoke.

"Toby, I hurt all over," she groaned quietly.

"It's okay." Toby said encouragingly, "We can rest for a while."

Toby made his sitting position more comfortable, as he cradled Gwen on his lap and waited for them both to feel strong enough to move on, while Emmie sat above in a tree, wondering why they had stopped.

They sat in silence as Toby rocked Gwen gently like a newborn baby. Gwen closed her eyes again and continued to groan softly, relaxing in his arms. Slowly, they began to drift off from exhaustion of all that had happened to them, when Toby heard faint voices coming from high up, not far from the ledge. Panic woke him from his semi-slumber, and he shook Gwen gently.

"We need to move on, Gwen," he whispered anxiously.

Reluctantly, she opened her eyes, "Oh, can't we rest here a bit longer?" Gwen was feeling better, but had been revelling in the comfort and warmth of his arms.

"Come on," Toby said determinedly, his command answering her question. He helped her to her feet. Then, taking her hand, walked purposefully deeper into the jungle.

⟫●⟪

As they walked along the path, Joe and Doreen each prayed silently for Toby and the girl, not wanting to think about what they might find when they reached the Alejate, but unbidden images of what they might find haunted them at every step. It seemed to take a lot longer than it had the previous day, and Joe wanted to yell at Rebeca and the others to move faster. The noises of the jungle and the annoying mosquitoes only served to make Joe more irritable and the knot in his stomach was like a spring being compressed down tighter and tighter until he thought he might explode. Joe covered his ears in desperation as the birds seemed to grow louder with their squawks and chirps and trills, and he had to use every last ounce of strength not to cry out for them all to be quiet.

Just then, a long root tripped him up and he stumbled forward. Joe threw out his arms to break his fall. A jolt of pain shot up his wrists and he called out in agony, swearing.

The group stopped and looked back to see what had happened and Doreen was torn between the surprise at his language and concern for her nephew. Seconds later, she was crouching beside him, one hand resting on his back comfortingly. Joe growled,

"I'm fine, let's just get going, Aunt Dor," he said, not hearing the gruffness in his voice above the taunting voices in his head:

"Toby's dead! Toby's dead!" Joe scrambled to his feet and stomped ahead of his distressed aunt as the group continued on.

Finally, they reached their destination and this time, Joe and Doreen were allowed to join Rebeca and her father as they approached chief Xochilt and his son Mundo who were sat under the same tree where they had spent the previous afternoon. They stood as Rebeca and the group approached him and Mundo smiled broadly at her in anticipation.

Rebeca lowered her head slightly in respect, while her father exchanged words with Xochilt. Rebeca turned back to Joe and Doreen to translate,

"We will go now to the sac ... the place where they left Toby and Gwen," Rebeca spoke softly, the dread in all of them almost tangible. She reached out to Joe who by now looked close to a meltdown, and held his right hand in hers, squeezing tenderly and looking compassionately into his eyes. Her touch immediately dissipated some of his anger and his shoulders sank slowly as he breathed out a slow sigh. He squeezed back in appreciation, then let go as the group turned to head down the path to discover Toby and Gwen's fate – and Rebeca's.

Joe was suddenly torn between wanting to hurry and not wanting to see the place in case his brother and the girl were not there. However, he had no choice as Mundo led the group at a quick pace, anxious to find Toby and Gwen safe, so that he might finally make Rebeca his wife. By the time they got to the ledge, they were all panting. Mundo arrived first and called out in anger as he saw the empty ledge, falling to his knees and pounding the ground fiercely.

"Oh!" Doreen gasped and held her hand to her mouth, frozen on the spot as she saw the empty, bloody ledge. "No!" She cried out and reached out to Joe who clung to her as they both began to sob.

Rebeca ran to the ledge, and stood looking intently. Xochilt and Mundo walked over to her as Lucio looked on. Mundo grabbed her by the shoulders and spoke imploringly to her. She shook her head from side to side and Mundo shouted. He turned to his father and pleaded with him, pointing back to Rebeca. Rebeca looked away from them and walked to the edge of the ledge, looking around thoughtfully.

As Xochilt and Mundo's interaction grew heated, Lucio walked over to Rebeca and put his arm around her protectively, drawing her back to the path. Joe and Doreen were frantic, and Joe started to walk towards Mundo with clenched fists hanging beside him. Rebeca trotted over to him and put her hand on his shoulder.

"Joe!" she spoke sharply. Startled out of his focused rage, he looked down at Rebeca who lowered her voice instinctively, even though the others did not speak English.

"They are not dead, Joe. Please, just come. Say nothing, please. Let us go and I will explain when we get back home." Joe struggled with his emotions, wanting desperately to believe her, but revenge still racing through his blood as he eyed the spears that the two men held.

Rebeca turned to Doreen and made eye contact, nodding and smiling slightly as she motioned for her to leave with them. Doreen immediately understood and responded as instructed, the four of them hurrying down the path with Xochilt and Mundo following close behind. When they got to the village, Rebeca remembered Toby's back pack. For some reason, she felt compelled to ask for its return.

The chief nodded his permission and called to a woman who was walking past at that moment. She nodded in submission and hurried off to the chief's hut. Shortly, she was back with Toby's backpack and the pile of clothes they had taken from Toby and Gwen.

"You stripped them?!" Doreen covered her face at the thought, as Rebeca received the backpack and clothes and held them tightly.

"It is okay, Doreen, I will explain everything when we get back. Let us go before Mundo grows angry again."

Obediently, Joe and Doreen followed Rebeca and her father as they marched quickly out of the village and back onto the jungle path. Several times, Joe and Doreen tried to ask Rebeca questions, but she kept asking them to wait. They all hurried along and made good time, soon arriving back at Rebeca and her father's village. Benito was nowhere to be seen.

Rebeca asked them to sit down in the middle of the village beside some women who were preparing some kind of vegetable. Young children ran and played while some older ones helped the women. Joe and Doreen looked expectantly at Rebeca, waiting for her explanation. She smiled broadly before speaking.

"I could see where two people had gone down the steep hill – Mundo and his father were too cross to notice. I am certain that Toby and Gwen have escaped, but I am not sure what condition they will be in." She paused, taking in a deep breath and letting it out slowly as she thought things through in her mind. "We will eat to strengthen ourselves, then we will go back and find them. They will be tired, they will not go far. We will find them today, I am sure." Rebeca was sat next to Doreen and she grabbed her hand gently and gave it a comforting squeeze. Doreen and Joe were slightly comforted, but still consumed with worry.

"Are you sure you will be able to find them?" asked Joe, "Shouldn't we have gone to find them straight away?"

Rebeca shook her head. "Mundo was following us home for quite a while. He was very reluctant to let me go."

Joe raised an eyebrow. "Mundo was following us?"

"Yes," Rebeca said. "He was not very careful." Her face beamed as she continued, "Not only am I better at fishing than him, I am better at tracking and knowing when I am being tracked!

Joe let out a slow, soft whistle, "No wonder he wants you as his wife: you are amazing!"

Rebeca bent her head down slightly and blushed, making Joe want to wrap his arms around her. He had never met any girl like Rebeca.

Rebeca walked quickly over to her grandmother, talking in her native tongue, before turning and trotting up the steps to her hut. Her grandmother called out to a couple of children, motioning with her hands, and they scurried off while she put some more wood on the fire. She took the big cooking pot and hung it on the hook over the fire, then poured liquid from a nearby jug.

Exhausted, Joe and Doreen collapsed by the fire. Doreen sitting down, while Joe crouched down beside her. He suddenly remembered Benito, and he almost snarled as he spoke,

"I wonder where that little snake is?"

Doreen looked over at him, frowning. "Joe, you must let go of this hatred. It will only eat away at your heart."

"Some people deserve to be hated, Aunt Doreen." Joe picked up a branch off the ground and started pulling it apart forcefully.

"What has happened to you, Joe?" Doreen said worriedly. "You used to be more compassionate; kinder." She put a hand on his shoulder and he fought the temptation to brush it off. He was getting fed up with Doreen, but he did not want to disrespect her. He really could not see how she could be so kind to someone so weak and totally lacking in any positive qualities. Even Mundo had the positive qualities of determination and courage. A sharp arrow of conscience pierced him. What *had* happened to him? He stood up suddenly and Doreen looked up at him questioningly.

"I think I'll go for a little walk … to clear my head," Joe mumbled, and strode off down along the river.

"Don't go far, sweetheart." Doreen called out after him.

Moments later, Rebeca burst out of her hut, transformed back into her former self, with her hair pulled back in one long braid down her back. She wore beige loose fitting cotton trousers topped by a bright pink cotton blouse. Purposefully, she trotted down the steps in her simple leather sandals, and over to help her grandmother prepare the meal.

———⇒»●«⇐———

GWEN and TOBY

After about half an hour, Gwen began stumbling as Toby continued to pull her along at a quick pace, and finally he stopped, looking at her compassionately. He listened carefully. The jungle was amazingly noisy with the calls of the birds and the chatters of the monkeys and all the other animals, but he strained hard to listen for people talking. He decided they were probably safe to stop for a while.

"We can rest for a bit," he smiled at Gwen as she scowled up at him before collapsing on the ground in a sitting position. He lowered himself down beside her, and was startled as Emmie hurled herself between them. Toby grinned as he scratched Emmie's belly and she curled up on his lap, busying herself with preening her fur. He kissed the top of her head and she looked up at him with a squeaky grin.

"Yuck!" Gwen wrinkled her face. "That thing probably has fleas! I can't believe you let it on your lap, let alone *kiss* it!"

Toby raised an eyebrow as he looked at Gwen, muddied with soil and dried blood still in her hair and smeared down her face. "I kissed *you*, didn't I?" he laughed.

Gwen opened her mouth to speak, then looked down at herself. She touched her face and scraped at some crusted blood on her cheek with her fingernails. Her eyes filled with water and her bottom lip began to quiver and Toby was immediately sorry.

"Gwen, I uh…"

A loud CRACK interrupted Toby, and he jolted to the side as something whizzed passed his arm. Emmie screeched and leaped off his lap.

Tadeo! Toby grabbed Gwen's hand and yanked her to her feet, running in the opposite direction of the bullet. Gwen cried out as pain jolted down her shoulder from the force of Toby's pull, and she stumbled along behind him in panic. Terror raced through their bodies, spurring the teenagers on as another shot rang out, hitting a nearby tree. Emmie leapt back into the branches and swung along above, easily keeping up with them. She squealed and barked frantically, as though shouting at Tadeo who was cursing as he ran, waving his gun in front of him. He jerked to a stop and took another shot.

Crack! Gwen shrieked as a bullet nicked the top of her shoulder. "Toby! It hit me!"

Toby panicked and looked back at her as he continued to pull her along. Blood was running down her arm. His mind raced as his legs continued propelling them forward. How could they get away?!

Tadeo was about thirty metres behind them and just visible through the thick undergrowth. He was momentarily distracted by some long vines that hung down from the large trees. Toby scanned their surroundings, trying desperately to find a place to hide.

Suddenly, a huge boar/anteater-like creature burst through the bushes near Tadeo, quickly followed by several native men with spears, shouting at the screeching, snorting beast. One of them threw a spear and the animal let out a shrill whistle as it floundered to its knees, gasping for breath.

Toby and Gwen stood as if in a trance, watching the surreal scene as though it were on television. The men ran towards it and gathered around the poor animal as they cheered and shouted out in a foreign language, waving their spears and patting each other on the back.

Emmie barked sharply and Toby shook himself. Now was their chance to find somewhere to hide – but where? Frantically, Toby looked around for a means of escape. Something scurried past his feet and he jumped as he looked down to see a strange, reddish furry creature with a long nose and striped tail. He watched it snuffling as it hurried along to his right, then suddenly seemed to disappear into the ground. Instinctively, Toby dragged Gwen over to where he had last seen the creature. Moving back some large fern leaves, Toby stepped back as he nearly fell into a large, jagged hole in some stony ground. Carefully, he crouched down and looked in, immediately jerking upwards as the furry red creature poked his head up and jumped out passed him. It shuffled noisily through the undergrowth, searching the ground for a snack, oblivious to the commotion of the hunting natives and the furious gun toting man.

Toby watch him for a moment, then caught sight of Tadeo's head over the bushes distracted by the men and wondering whether to shoot or hide. Toby quickly turned and focused back on the hole. It was about eight feet deep and varied in width due to the rocks, three to four feet in diameter. Wide enough for the two of them.

In a split second, Toby grabbed the edge and silently swung himself down, landing on the damp, squidgy ground. Immediately, Gwen's face appeared over the edge. Toby held his hands up to her.

"Hurry, Gwen," he hissed, "before Tadeo sees you!" Without question, she quickly parted the leaves and lowered herself gingerly backwards over the sharp edge. Toby grabbed her by the waist, gently easing her to the damp ground. He put his finger to his lips as she started to speak. Their hearts beat loudly as they heard some rustling in the vegetation above them, and Toby nearly cried out as something landed gently on his head. Little fingers grabbed his ears and he smiled as he took Emmie down and gave her a cuddle.

"My shoulder is killing me, Toby," Gwen whispered tearfully as she held her left hand over her grazed right shoulder. Toby looked down at Gwen and saw the blood trickling down between her fingers. He broke off a leaf from a plant that was growing out of the side of the rocks and lifted her hand as he wiped the blood from the wound. Gwen flinched and Toby mouthed, "Sorry." The bullet had taken off several layers of skin, about 5mm wide, where it had brushed the top of her collar bone. He ripped off another couple of leaves and rolled them up, making a compress and holding it down carefully on the injury, trying to stop the flow. Gwen looked up and thanked him with her smile. While he held the leaves with one hand, he put his other arm around her. She was shivering, from the pain and the fear and the cold damp surroundings, so he drew her closer. Despite the fact that she was sharing Toby's embrace with the 'flea infested creature', she was comforted and she breathed deeply against his warm chest.

They stood for some time, listening to what sounded like the loud dying breath of the large animal, and the shouts and laughter of the men. Slowly, the raucous frivolity of the hunting party lessened.

Finally, Gwen whispered, "I need to sit down, Toby, my legs are aching." Toby's eyes had adjusted to the diminished light around him and he scanned the walls of their refuge. There was a small outcrop of flat rock that was just large enough for someone to sit on. He motioned for Gwen to sit, but as soon as her bottom touched the cold surface, she squealed and jumped back up.

Toby's finger darted to his lips as he hissed, "Shhhh!"

Tears filled her eyes. His harsh tone was the last thing she needed when she was scared and her shoulder was hurting. Toby sighed. "I'm sorry," he whispered. "Here."

He sat down on the ledge and opened his arms, motioning for her to sit on his lap. She crouched down gratefully into a sitting position. They were both shivering, but they drew warmth from each other and Emmie. Toby was feeling quite exhausted, and as he wrapped his arms around her, he gently rested his head on the top of hers. He really did not know how much more he could take. All he wanted to do was curl up into a ball like the little monkey that now had her eyes closed as she dozed between the two of them.

Above the hole, they could hear the men still laughing and chattering happily. It sounded like they were eating the animal. The thought of eating raw meat repulsed Toby, but despite himself, his stomach growled and Gwen's made gurgling noises in response.

"I'm hungry, Toby," she said needlessly.

"Ya, so am I."

He looked down at Emmie who slept contentedly. He guessed she had fed herself somewhere along their travels. Or maybe she didn't need to eat as often as humans. Toby thought about the last meal he had had with his parents. It was a couple of home made pizzas – a Hawaiian and a pepperoni; and there was garlic bread. He had still been annoyed with them for sending him off to Canada and ruining his summer, so he had decided to refuse to show any enjoyment, despite the fact that the food was quite delicious.

Toby wondered what his Aunty Doreen and Uncle Derrick were doing, since Tadeo's phone call. Were they looking for him? What was Benito doing? His thoughts returned to his current surroundings: was Tadeo still standing there watching the men? ... Toby's thoughts quickly grew more and more random. Fatigue overcame them both and eventually sleep engulfed them into shivering, fitful dreams.

A little way beyond the hole, the men had cut out the heart and the liver, smearing the blood across their faces and chests. After cutting off one of the hind legs, they shared it between them as they recounted the hunt with great enjoyment.

None of them had noticed the man with angry blue eyes standing several paces away with a gun in his hand, crouching behind a large bush, watching them impatiently. Tadeo looked beyond them where Toby and the girl had been. He swore and frowned deeply. They had disappeared. If only these natives would just take their feast back to their village. His legs began to ache and he looked around. Right beside him on his left, a tree had fallen over. He carefully moved to sit down on it, making great effort to be silent. Though, he thought angrily, they were making so much noise with their hunting rituals that they probably wouldn't hear him if he had called out to them. He sighed deeply, stretching his neck up so he could see above the bushes. He scanned the area carefully, memorizing where he had last seen the two kids. They wouldn't have gone far, he was sure. Once these annoying men left, he would begin a thorough search. The thought of killing them all entered his mind. It would be easy enough – but he didn't have enough bullets left for them and the teenagers. And he wanted to make sure the kids didn't escape.

However, time ticked slowly on, and the men continued with their feasting and loud boasting of their skill in the hunt. He did not understand the language, but by the laughter and the joking noises and pats on the back, he was quite sure that that was what they were doing. He gritted his teeth, getting more and more furious. Why wouldn't they just go!?!

Tadeo held the gun sideways, tapping it impatiently against his chest. He felt the cold metal with his palm and ran his fingertips along the smooth metal barrel of his 1911 colt 45. He loved the feel of the gun. It made him feel powerful. Strong. In control. His fingers ran along the beautiful, sleek cocobolo handle. It was his favourite gun. Not just because it was such an exquisite gun to look at. He loved the seven shot clip, and his entire body tingled with each bullet that burst forth, straining to reach its target. When it met its target, when it entered flesh, the satisfaction he felt was euphoric. Tadeo's eyes glazed over in excitement at the thought. His wife, Maria, had called him a psychopath. Many times. And then again, one last time as she headed out the door, never to be seen again.

He spit on the ground in disgust at the thought of her. He was better on his own. She asked far too many questions. And when he condescended to answer the repeated questions of where he had been, she had the audacity not to believe him. So what if it was a lie. She still had no right not to believe him. She had no proof! He growled to himself. Women!

He woke from his daydream as the hunters prepared to carry the tapir back to their waiting tribe. One of the men took his large, razor sharp machete and hacked down a young tree with one swipe. Tadeo flinched, despite himself. It almost matched the power of his revolver.

The other men cut down some vines and tied the animal's remaining three feet to the trunk. When they had gathered their spears, one man positioned himself at the front and the other at the hind end of the beast and the two hoisted the tree on their shoulders with the animal hanging down between them. Still jovial, the men turned and, *finally,* thought Tadeo, headed back through the jungle in the direction from which they had stampeded. This time, though, they sauntered happily, still talking loudly and laughing heartily.

Tadeo stood and watched for a moment, waiting until he could no longer hear them, then turned and focused on where he had last seen the two kids. Clicking on the safety catch, he stuffed the barrel into the front of his jeans and, parting the branches in front of him, strode forward, confident that they were still close by and he would soon finish the job, and search them for the diamonds his nephew had probably passed to them. Then he would catch that monkey and finally, sort out getting his stupid nephew back, from wherever he was!

CHAPTER 19

Toby was suddenly aware of the quiet drifting down from the top of the hole – if you could ever call the jungle quiet – and he felt certain the hunters had left. His heart started beating heavily as he realized that this meant Tadeo would again start hunting them. Gwen sensed his body tense, and she looked up at him. He put his finger to his lips, not daring to make even the slightest bit of noise. Emmie's brown eyes looked up at him searchingly, and he smiled despite the danger. She silently tucked herself further under his arm as she sensed his fear. Not to be outdone, Gwen snuggled in closer as well, and Toby did his best to accommodate the two of them. His ears strained to hear what was going on above the hole. He could hear someone in the distance stomping through the undergrowth, and the noise was quickly getting closer.

"It's no good hiding!" shouted Tadeo in a gruff voice. "I'll look under every fern and behind every bush until I find you! I am NOT leaving until I get those diamonds!" A sinister grin spread across his face. "And my gun has a bit of lead left in it that needs to find a home!" He threw his head back at his joke, and the three fugitives shivered at his words involuntarily. Gwen squeezed Toby's side, as if the action would somehow save her. Toby struggled for breath under her tight embrace and Emmie made some little gasping noises, poking her little face up between them. Amazingly, she seemed to know to keep quiet. Toby could hear her tiny heart beating quickly and wondered if monkeys hearts always beat fast or if she was actually frightened. Did she know they were in danger?

Tadeo kept shouting out threats and profanities, his voice growing louder and then quieter again. Toby guessed he was doing a sweep back and forth, as he heard the man knocking back bushes and plants that got in his way.

Suddenly, Tadeo burst out in loud laughter, "I think I'll just sit and wait here for you – you'll eventually move, and THEN I'll find you! Ha! Ha!"

Tadeo spotted another tree trunk lying on its side, and sat down, crossing his arms across his chest with the gun held tightly in his hand.

Split! Splat! Drops of rain hit Toby's arm, and he bit his lip. Hopefully it would only be a light shower.

At that thought, the heavens opened and it felt like a hosepipe had been turned on them full blast. Toby leaned forward over Gwen and Emmie to shelter them and they tucked themselves underneath him. The rain poured down and the two teenagers were completely drenched within minutes, while the little monkey managed to stay dry.

Emmie suddenly poked her head out between them and jumped up a few feet. Toby looked up and saw a little hole in the side of the rock, just big enough for a small capuchin. She curled herself up into a ball and looked down at him, grinning her cheesy smile at him. He smiled lopsidedly despite himself.

Still the rain fell heavily, a puddle growing on the ground which quickly covered the bottom of their hideout and then began creeping steadily up the sides. The water very soon covered their feet completely and they began to shiver uncontrollably, despite holding each other closely for warmth.

Tadeo laughed heartily. "I don't mind the rain. I love it! I can sit in this all day! I'm betting that little wimpy nina won't last long!" He paused. "Actually, after what you two have been through, I bet it will finish you both off! Perhaps you'll both catch pneumonia and die. That will save me some bullets! Ha! Ha!" He guffawed, lifting his shirt and tucking his gun underneath, into his trousers.

Still the rain came down heavily and the pool in the hole continued to rise. Gwen lifted up her feet and curled herself into a ball on Toby's lap, while he left his feet where they were, with the water now at his ankles. He could feel it, millimetre by millimetre, crawling up his legs like a living being and although it was not very cold, he began to shiver. The warmth from Gwen's body nestled on his lap and in his arms comforted him, but a chill seemed to be creeping out from within him, like a jellyfish slowly unfolding its tentacles and reaching out in all directions. Half conscious, Toby leaned his cold cheek gently on top of Gwen's shorn head, nuzzling down to the warmth of her scalp, and as the water tickled up his shins, he involuntarily drew Gwen even closer, like he was clutching a hot water bottle. A little smile curled the edges of her lips as she misinterpreted his actions.

The minutes ticked slowly by, and Toby flitted in and out of consciousness. When the water began lapping against his bare knees, he was back at the Cornish seaside when he was six years old.

It was the fifth day of their holiday, and still the skies were grey. It had been raining off and on all week, so they had gone to museums and indoor activities of various descriptions, but they only had one more day there, and he and his brother wanted to spend some time on the beach. At least it was empty! His parents were behind him snuggled together under a blanket, and sheltered beneath a beach umbrella, flapping its edges in the gentle breeze. His brother wandered down a little way along the beach, collecting seashells and interesting things that had turned up on the wet sand.

Toby had been drawn to the salty waves and sat with his legs outstretched, as the water crawled towards him in a rhythm, back and forth, back and forth. Slowly coming a little closer with each wave, until it reached his toes. He felt hypnotized by the motion, and the tickling of the waters. Each time, being fooled that the water was rolling away from him.

Rolling, rolling, rolling, until, "Crash!", another wave would break its retreat and pull it back towards him: urging the water, drawing it closer and sliding further up his legs like a cool, soft blanket.

"Aargh!!"

The two of them jumped as Tadeo stood in anger and his loud voice boomed across the forest floor and down the hole; his actions belying his claims of patience and, like a toddler with a dangerous toy, shot off a couple of his precious bullets randomly into the trees, scattering little squealing monkeys and birds in various directions.

"Okay!" he shouted furiously, as he turned slowly around, his squinted eyes scanning the bushes, desperately trying to see some sign of his prey. "You can just rot out here! I'll come back in a few days and find you easily from the stench of your decaying bodies!" He laughed angrily, as his piercing blue eyes gave another detailed sweep of the area before heading back in the direction he had come.

Gwen looked up at Toby and whispered, "Can we get out yet?" He shook his head and put his finger to his lips, then held up his hand, holding out five fingers, and closing them, then opening them again slowly. His hands felt stiff, almost painful.

She nodded reluctantly, as the water crept over Toby's knees and began tapping her bottom and feet. Gwen fidgeted, trying in vain to keep out of the water, as she held on to Toby's neck, pulling herself upwards. She glanced up at Emmie, who had her eyes closed, dry and snuggled in a tight ball in her little hole. She actually looked quite happy and comfortable, much to Gwen's annoyance.

At that thought, the rain began falling even heavier, and the pool grew deeper, and Gwen began to panic as the water tapped her waist, then ground water began pouring over the edges, adding volumes to the water in their hole.

Toby was back at the beach in Cornwall and he thrashed in alarm as a large wave swept over him, knocking him over. Standing up suddenly, he dislodged Gwen who cried out and grabbed him desperately as she scrambled to find her footing in the deep water.

Toby's glazed eyes stared in her direction before he saw her, then he shook himself into a dazed consciousness as she began crying. He was so tired, and the water pressed itself against him, weighing him down, but he clawed against the rocky soil wall, pulling himself to a standing position on the shelf where he had been sitting. Gwen clambered clumsily up, as he lent down and pulled her to a standing position beside him. The water was now at her chest, and he saw her terrified face as she looked up at him with her teeth chattering. Closing his eyes, and gathering what strength that was left inside of him, he cupped his hands for her to stand on and hoisted her upwards towards the entrance of the hole. She grabbed the greenery hanging over the edge and pulled herself up as Toby lifted.

His knees quivered as the exertion overwhelmed him and he began to crumple, slipping off the edge of the rock and sinking down as the water enveloped him.

"Toby!" Gwen screamed as her head poked over the lip of the hole and saw Toby collapsing. He coughed and spluttered as her cry reached his ears and the water reached his nostrils at the same time. His his eyes shot open. The adrenaline was just enough to help him back onto the rock, and he stood up, steadying himself as he grabbed onto the rocks and soil that lined the side. Emmie's little eyes peered down out of her nook and she chattered down at him as though she were encouraging him.

He breathed deeply several times, then stretching his arms upwards, he strained to reach as high as he could. His fingers just reached the top. He grabbed the edge and inhaled deeply before bending his knees slightly and propelling himself upwards, straining to release the grasp of the water on his tired body. Unfortunately, his left hand lost its grip and he swung to his right, losing his balance and falling back with a splash. Gwen screamed again and leaned down further, as Toby thrashed about, gasping for breath while his feet flailed below him, finally locating the rock so he could stand up. The rain had begun to let up, but he was still surrounded by the heavy wet blanket that was pulling him downwards.

Leaning against the side, he pressed his cheek against the sodden rocky soil, willing it to cling to him. He closed his eyes tightly, and called out through clenched teeth.

"Please, God! Help me! I ... just ... can't ... do it!" He could hear Gwen weeping into her hands as she curled herself up into a ball somewhere above him, no longer able to look; not wanting to watch him disappear beneath the murky surface.

Slowly, he felt a faint warmth filtering through his fingers and toes and creeping up his legs and arms before filling his entire body. He stood up straight, and reached high, again grabbing the edges with his fingers tightly and, before the strength could leave his hands, he took one deep breath and, mustering every last shred of energy within him, jumped up, his aching arms dragging out his torso onto the grass, as his legs dangled beneath him in the hole.

Gwen startled at the sound and jumped to his rescue, leaning over and hauling his legs out so he lay outstretched on the ground. Then she immediately threw herself on top of him and wrapped her arms around him in her joy. The sudden weight on his chest made Toby gasp, and Gwen rolled off, leaving one arm across his chest as she lay tightly beside him.

At that moment, the rain stopped and a thin ray of hot sun poked through the dark canopy, touching Toby on the cheek. Gwen smiled and gently touched the warmth with her fingertip, as Toby disappeared once again into unconsciousness.

CHAPTER 20

LUCIO'S TRIBE

Joe returned just as Rebeca and her grandmother began dishing out the delicious smelling stew. Doreen looked up at him as he strode towards her. His face was still brooding, so she decided to say nothing as he sat beside her and they both accepted their bowls from some young smiling children who were distributing the food.

They ate quickly, in silence, impatient to get going and find Toby. Benito, as before, was happy to sit back and enjoy his food; though he did keep glancing over at Joe, who seemed to now, thankfully, be ignoring him.

Fifteen minutes later, everyone was finished and the children gathered all their bowls. Benito surreptitiously snuck back into the hut, just in case someone should remember he was there and ask him to go along.

He needn't have worried, as Rebeca was only planning on taking Joe and Doreen. Really, she only needed Joe – in case Gwen or Toby were injured – but she knew Doreen would not be dissuaded from accompanying them.

Slinging a water bag over her shoulder, Rebeca only needed to look over at Joe and Doreen, and they jumped to their feet and followed her into the jungle.

At first, she took the path on which she had sent Toby and Gwen, and it was easy walking. However, after a little while, she veered off and headed into some thicker undergrowth where the going was slower. The large ferns whipped at Doreen and Joe's bare arms and they were both glad that they were wearing trousers instead of shorts. Joe shook his head in amazement as he looked down at Rebeca's bare feet clad only in simple sandals as she walked steadily in front of him, with the unkind vegetation slapping at her ankles. He supposed she was used to it and wondered if she could even go barefoot in the jungle.

After half an hour, Rebeca stopped at the base of a hill and pointed up. "That's where they were tied up and left."

Doreen and Joe looked up, and could just make out the edge of the stone hanging over the steep incline.

"How on earth did you know it was here? There was no path!" exclaimed Doreen in amazement.

Rebeca smiled, and answered humbly, "Don't forget I grew up in this jungle. Just like you could find your way around a large city, if you grew up in one."

Rebeca looked around her, envisioning Toby and Gwen as they came down the hill. "Hmmmm," she thought silently to herself, "One of them fell most of the way. I hope they are both all right." Inadvertently, she frowned deeply and Joe caught the worried expression.

"What's the matter?" he asked.

Not wanting to worry them any more, and not really being able to tell the extent of the harm that might have come to the one that fell, she relaxed her face and said encouragingly with a grin, "They walk heavily! I could track them in my sleep."

Joe looked at her and, yet again, wondered in amazement at the abilities of this intriguing young woman.

Just as Rebeca took a step in the direction that Toby and Gwen had headed, the heavens opened, and she instinctively glanced around, herding Joe and his aunt into a little enclave at the bottom of the hill.

As they huddled together in the confined space, Joe wondered if Rebeca would still be able to track Toby and this girl after a heavy rain. Surely it would cover all their tracks. He opened his mouth to speak then closed it, feeling an overwhelming confidence in her abilities.

None of them spoke as the rain fell loudly. It was a strange transition from the cacophony of the jungle animals and birds to the deafening roar of the rain battering the leaves as it crashed down through the canopy and deluged their surroundings.

There seemed to be no let up of the rain, and Doreen began to wonder if they were wasting precious time trying to stay dry when they should be trying to find her nephew. She glanced at Rebeca questioningly, who in answer to Doreen's thoughts, spoke just loud enough to be heard above the storm.

"It is okay, Doreen. I will still be able to track them. Their footsteps will be mostly washed away, but the plants where they walked will still guide me. We will wait until the rain stops, as it will be easier for me to see.

Doreen nodded, accepting her answer but still apprehensive at the wait, desperate to find Toby. And this girl. Doreen wondered about her parents and how much they must be worrying. At least she and Joe knew the teenagers were alive and walking; *and* they were getting close to them, she told herself. They MUST be getting near.

"Oh please God!" She pleaded silently for the hundredth time. "Please help us find them soon! And please help them both be all right!"

Joe was growing exceedingly restless and his impatience was feeding the brooding darkness at the pit of his stomach that was beginning to grow, spreading upwards into his heart. It beat harder and faster as the waiting continued, and just as he felt he could stand it no longer, the rain stopped and they immediately all stepped out into the open. At once, the orchestra of the jungle again began to play around them, as the three people fell into position, Rebeca leading the way, with Joe close at her heels and Doreen at the rear.

Doreen and Joe were surprised to find that the ground was not as soggy as they felt it should have been. Presumably, all the plants and trees soaked up the water willingly, leaving very little lying on top of the ground.

They moved forward quickly, as Rebeca again commented on how heavy footed Toby and Gwen were. In fact, Joe and Doreen felt that they were walking as fast as they had been before they reached the point where Rebeca had picked up their tracks.

Suddenly, Rebeca stopped, and put her hand up. Doreen and her nephew looked at her questioningly, saying nothing as she put a finger to her mouth.

A few moments later, Doreen and Joe heard it. Someone stomping through the jungle grumbling angrily to himself. So enraged was he, that he did not notice Rebeca and the others until he was virtually on top of them.

Looking up in a startled fury, he shouted, "HA! You're looking for those brats! Well, it's too late!"

Doreen gasped in horror, waiting for him to continue, but not wanting to hear his words, anticipating more unbearable news.

"I shot them both and left them for the jaguar!" His evil laugh reverberated through his chest and as Joe stepped forwards, Tadeo pointed his gun, stopping Joe in his tracks. He had no bullets left, but he wasn't about to let this rescue team go further into the jungle to find the teenagers. That Rebeca was a smart girl, she would be able to find them.

As the group stood there, Tadeo's cunning mind thought quickly. If only he could keep them from going into the jungle until the next day, he was sure those kids would be dead. But he could not risk going back to Lucio's village. It was now early afternoon. If he could hold them off until dark, they would have to wait until morning to go back and try and find their friends.

Without warning, the rumbling volcano of emotions inside Joe erupted in a torrent of ferocity and he lunged at the madman who was standing between him and his brother. His unexpected movement caught Tadeo off guard so, while normally he could have tackled Joe, he stumbled backwards and the two fell together with a thud. In the same movement, Joe grabbed the gun from Tadeo's clenched hand and tossed it to the side. Rebeca saw it land and grabbed it without hesitation, pointing it at Tadeo. She looked bemused as he laughed at her in a pained breath, having had the wind knocked out of him when he landed.

"It's ... empty."

She frowned, not trusting him. Pointing the gun away from them, she pulled the trigger. Nothing happened. He was telling the truth. The group realized he probably had been lying about killing Toby and Gwen, to stop them from going to find the teenagers. Doreen began to cry from relief and the worry that had filled her entire body. Rebeca tossed down the gun and she turned to Doreen, hugging her tightly.

"Let's ... get moving and ... find Toby." Joe slowly sat up, wiping some blood from his mouth with the back of his hand. Rebeca nodded and breathed deeply. Trying to focus herself, she looked around slowly, then moved forward as she found the tracks. Joe gathered his strength and stood, following Rebeca and avoiding Doreen's sad gaze as she began walking behind them, leaving an angry Tadeo sitting on the jungle floor. His pride was severely wounded at the thought that he had let the young man overpower him.

It was difficult at first, because Tadeo's movements were mixed with Toby and Gwen's, but finally they split into two distinct tracks, and Rebeca's pace increased as she followed the two teenagers tracks.

She stopped short as she spotted the blood from the tapir. She bent down and touched it with her fingertip as she looked around the kill site. A large animal had been hunted and killed here, not humans. Standing up again, she turned to Doreen and Joe.

"A hunt has ended here. It was recent. Probably this morning." She paused, then called out in a loud voice, "Toby! Gwen! Toby! Gwen!" All three of them listened carefully.

"Help! Over here!" Gwen had dozed off from exhaustion, and she woke when she heard her name.

They ran towards the voice and Joe reached them first. Falling on his knees by his brother's side, Joe ignored the girl and focused his attention on Toby. He sighed with relief as he felt the warmth of his body. He was alive! Joe held his face in his hands. He wasn't just warm, he was hot. Doreen interrupted his thoughts as she knelt down beside her nephew.

"Is he all right?" she asked worriedly.

Rebeca turned her attention to Gwen whose eyes had filled with tears of relief. Rebeca hugged her tightly. "Can you walk?" Gwen nodded and managed to stand on her weak wobbly legs as she grasped Rebeca's offered hand.

"Something's wrong!" cried Joe. "He is shaking and I can't rouse him!" He looked to Rebeca, and Doreen's gaze followed his, both certain that she would know what was wrong and would be able to help.

As Rebeca bent down to examine Toby, Doreen took her place by Gwen's side and put her arm around the trembling girl. Just then, Toby moaned and held his stomach, his eyes remaining closed. Rebeca touched his face. He was very hot and his entire body was covered with sweat.

"I think he has malaria. We must get him back to our village where I can treat him with cinchona bark. Can you carry him, Joe?"

Without hesitation, Joe bent down and carefully lifted up Toby in his arms, cradling him like a baby. Toby had lost weight, but Joe quickly realized that although it seemed unkind, he would have to carry him in a fireman's lift if he was going to make it all the way back. Carefully, and with Rebeca's help, he repositioned his brother over his shoulder and Toby let out another moan.

"Sorry, Tobs, we gotta get you back to the village so Rebeca can make you feel better."

Rebeca turned to Gwen, "Are you well enough to walk all the way back?" she asked concerned, looking at Gwen, whom she could see was extremely pale.

Gwen nodded as her lip quivered. She did not trust her voice as emotion welled up in her throat. She was beyond exhausted, but being rescued and the prospect of soon returning home, renewed her strength enough to spur her on to walk the distance back to the village – however long that might be.

Again Rebeca led the way, although this time much slower, as Joe struggled along behind her with the weight of his brother, and Doreen walked beside Gwen, with an arm around her shoulder for both physical and mental support.

No one had the energy or inclination to speak on the journey back that seemed to take twice as long, but finally they reached the edge of the jungle and Joe stumbled up the steps of his hut and breathed a deep sigh as he lay his brother gently on the mat.

Doreen took Gwen into Rebeca's hut, as instructed, so she could rest there undisturbed. Gwen sank down on her mat thankfully. Doreen turned to ask if she wanted anything to eat or drink, but saw the girl was already fast asleep. She pulled a blanket over Gwen, and left the her resting to go check on her nephew.

Joe had stripped Toby down to his boxers and was mopping him down with a cloth in a bucket of water that had been brought by one of the children as requested by Rebeca, while she went off to ground the cinchona bark and dissolve it into a liquid. She soon returned with a wooden cup, half full of the medicine.

"Keep him still while I try and get him to drink this." Rebeca directed Joe as she knelt beside Toby. Seeing Doreen, Rebeca nodded at her.

"Perhaps you can come over and speak to him. A familiar voice might enter his unconsciousness and help him to swallow. It is important for him to drink the whole amount that I have made."

Toby was moving back and forth fitfully and Joe was having difficulty holding him still. Doreen nodded and obediently crouched down at Toby's head and stroked his hair. "Toby, sweetheart," she spoke softly, "Toby, we need you to drink this, it will make you feel better." He moaned and tossed his head from side to side, sweat dripping off of him.

She tried again, speaking louder, praying she could reach deep into where his consciousness had retreated. "Toby, it's Aunty Doreen." She leaned over and kissed his wet forehead. Tears welled up in her eyes and she swallowed hard. "Can you hear me? Please, darling, you need to take this medicine."

For a brief moment, Toby stopped thrashing and he mumbled something unintelligible. Rebeca seized her moment and put the cup to his lips, pouring the liquid in. At first, he coughed as it reached the back of his throat, and Doreen encouraged him.

"Try, Toby, please swallow. Drink it down. Remember when you were a little boy and Mommy gave you medicine that tasted bad? Remember? Now Aunty Doreen wants you to drink some medicine that will make you feel better."

Swallow.

Rebeca poured more in his mouth.

Cough. Sputter. Mumble. Swallow.

"You were very poorly and you had to take some yucky tasting medicine. But it made you feel better. Do you remember sweetheart?"

Rebeca slowly drained the cup into Toby's mouth as Doreen encouraged him. "That's it, Toby, keep drinking. Come on, you'll feel better soon. Keep drinking."

Finally, the cup was finished. Rebeca stood up and stepped back, so Joe could continue wiping Toby down. Doreen sat by her nephew, stroking his head, not wanting to leave him.

"Come, Doreen," said Rebeca gently, "you must have some refreshment. You have not eaten much over the last couple of days."

Doreen thought to herself, her little amount of eating had actually been ever since she had heard Benito tell his story. Food had been the last thing on her mind, and she was still not hungry. The relief at finding Toby had immediately dissipated when they realized he was ill. She sighed deeply. There seemed to be nothing else to do but wait. So she stood and followed Rebeca out of the hut and down the wooden steps.

Rebeca led her to a log and motioned for her to sit down, then went over to where a pot was bubbling over the fire. Taking a bowl from the pile that was beside the fire, she dipped it in the pot, and gave the nourishing stew to Doreen. Rebeca then turned and repeated her actions before heading back into the hut with a bowl for Joe.

"Here, you too must take food." She took the cloth from Joe's hand and dropped it into the bucket. "Sit down and rest."

Joe, overwhelmed by the last few days, obeyed her soothing voice and sat down beside his brother. He looked up at Rebeca as she handed him the bowl of food. Her dark brown eyes held such kindness and compassion that he was filled with the warmth that emanated from them.

"Thank you," he spoke quietly, and she blushed as his gaze lingered and he squeezed her hand gently, not wanting to relinquishing his hold on her soft hand.

"When you have finished, you must go in your hut and lie down. And your aunt, as well. You are both exhausted and no more can be done for Toby for the moment. She broke off from his gaze and he released her hand as she looked at Toby, who had stopped moaning, and was now only slightly restless.

"I have mixed in some medicine that will bring down his temperature and help him to rest deeper. It will aid in his recovery. It will be about twenty-four hours before we know if the cinchona will help him."

At the thought that there might be more trouble ahead for his brother, panic rose in Joe's eyes, and Rebeca quickly added, "There is a doctor in Tudela that uses western medicine. If Toby is not responding to the bark by tomorrow afternoon, I will go and bring him here." She smiled comfortingly, "But please do not worry, I am sure that I will not have to. This medicine is very effective for malaria."

Rebeca sat down beside Joe, slightly further away than he would have liked. Neither of them spoke as Joe slowly ate his food, tasting nothing, but knowing that Rebeca was right and he needed to eat.

A short while later, Joe and Doreen were on their mats in their hut, resting in the cool from the early evening sun, still neither able to sleep. Rebeca was going to stay and watch him, and she had promised them that she would let them know if there was any change. She pulled the other mat closer to Toby so she could hear his breathing and monitor the fever through the night without having to get up to check on him.

Rebeca lay awake for quite a while listening, as Toby's breathing became less laboured. Soon it was barely audible. She reached out and touched his face. It was still warm, but had cooled considerably. She let her hand rest on his arm and she drifted off to sleep with her heart beating a little faster than normal.

Half an hour later, when it had become dark, she was still asleep, and did not see or hear the slender dark figure quietly creep in and grab the backpack by Toby's feet, then tiptoe quietly back out again. Neither did she hear an unhappy little capuchin making little sad squeaking noises in a nearby tree.

Just before the sun rose, Rebeca woke for the fourth time to check on Toby. His temperature had returned to normal, but he was still unconscious. She was unsure if the malaria was leaving him, or if it was still the effects of the drug she had given him. She lay back down, looking out through the window and watching the sky grow quickly lighter.

"SQUEAK!! SQUEAK!!"

She jumped up at the frantic cry. It was Emmie – something was wrong!" She ran down the steps outside and around the side of the hut just in time to see Benito, Tadeo, and a caged Emmie disappear into the jungle. Her heart sank. Poor Benito – he had thought that he had finally escaped his uncle. And poor Toby would be devastated that Emmie had been taken, most likely to be sold to someone in America.

As she turned back towards the hut, Doreen and Joe came out of their hut. "What was that?!" Joe turned to her questioningly.

"Benito and Emmie," she said sadly.

"Emmie?" asked Doreen.

"A very good friend of Toby's." She explained. They both looked at her confused, so she added, "a monkey." Forgetting Benito for the moment, at the mention of Toby's name, their thoughts immediately turned to him.

"How is Toby?" they asked in unison, as they both trotted down their steps and headed towards Toby's hut. Rebeca followed close behind, and as she reached the bottom of the steps, she noticed Toby's bag lying there with the zip open.

"That's funny," she thought, "I was sure we put it by his bed." She shrugged her shoulders, "I wonder how it got there?" The thought of Toby pushed the matter out of her head and she turned her attention to Joe and Doreen's question. "The fever is gone for now," she said cautiously, as she entered and stood beside Doreen and Joe.

"For now? You mean it might come back?" Joe bent down beside his brother and touched his forehead with the back of his hand, pleased that it felt so much cooler. Doreen crouched as well, and held Toby's hand in hers.

"Yes. It could be just the medicine for the fever that is working, rather than the malaria leaving him." She looked at Joe and then Doreen before adding, "But it is a good sign. He is resting now, and that will help his body to heal. Come and have some breakfast," she encouraged them.

Doreen chuckled despite herself, "You have a thing about feeding us!"

Rebeca smiled, and reluctantly the two of them followed her out to have something to eat and drink.

As they were finishing, Joe looked around him carefully.

"Where is Benito? That little weasel is usually not far from the food." He made a face and Doreen frowned at him.

"I guess you did not hear me earlier. Emmie and Benito both have been taken by Benito's uncle, Tadeo, the man we met in the jungle," answered Rebeca.

"Well, good riddance to bad rubbish," frowned Joe as he finished his breakfast.

Doreen and Rebeca looked at each other and shook their heads at Joe's lack of compassion for the boy. Joe just scowled and stood up.

"I'm going for a little walk and a wash in the river." And with that, he strode off, surprised that he was disturbed by Rebeca's response. Her disapproval niggled him, but he could not bring himself to sympathize with Benito.

Rebeca turned to Doreen. "Tell me about where you live," she said with an eagerness in her eyes. Doreen smiled.

"Well, it is certainly tamer than it is here!" Rebeca looked confused.

"Tamer?" she asked. "I do not understand."

"Well, we don't have dangerous animals or dangerous men trying to kill us! Nothing much exciting happens where I live. Life in Okotoks may be considered boring really, if you compared it to here!"

Rebeca nodded slightly, contemplating. "Perhaps," she bit her lip thoughtfully, imagining things that she had heard about the world beyond the small area of her life experience. She had never even been to Managua. "I would like one day, to visit…" she paused, trying to remember the name, then spoke slowly, "Ok … o … toks." A faraway look appeared in Rebeca's eyes. "There are many places I would like to see. My mother used to tell me about her country, England. I would also very much like to visit there."

A soft moan coming from Toby's hut turned both their heads, and they stood quickly, leaving the dishes on the ground in a hurry to check on him. Rebeca reached him first and bent down at his side, resting the palm of her hand on his cheek. Toby opened his eyes and looked up at her confused, then shut them again, weary from the effort.

"How is he?" Doreen asked anxiously, trusting in Rebeca's knowledge of the disease, despite her young age. Rebeca smiled.

"The fever is leaving him. I will give him some more medicine mixed with some coconut milk to give his body what it needs to heal, but I am confident he will be well. The disease will have weakened him greatly, though, so it will take a few days for him to recover completely and regain all his strength."

Doreen sighed deeply with relief, and leaned over her nephew, kissing his forehead. She paused for a moment, then suddenly remembered Gwen. "I'll go check on that young girl," Doreen said and, with her fears for Toby subsided, went to care for the other teenager.

She watched Doreen leave, then Rebeca turned back to Toby, drawing herself closer, and stroking his cheek, letting her fingers tips run across the sparse youthful beard that was attempting to show itself. Again, her heart gave a little quiver, and a sadness entered, knowing he would soon be leaving.

Toby opened his eyes again, and she immediately withdrew her hand, leaning back from her close position. He blinked a few times, taking in the face that was beside him. He felt he should know her, but for some reason, his mind was finding it difficult to process his surroundings. His body felt incredibly heavy and weak, and he struggled to reach into his brain to remember where he was. He started to panic, but the calm, comforting smile of the girl reassured him, and he made an attempt to smile back. He was amazed at the effort that it took. What was wrong with him?

"You have malaria," the girl spoke in a gentle voice, "but you are better now. I will get you some more medicine." She stood to go, and Toby panicked, grabbing her hand.

"Don't leave me!" Rebeca paused for a moment, enjoying his touch, then reluctantly took his hand off her arm.

"I will be right back." Within moments, she returned with the mixture and helped him to lean over to drink it. He drank thirstily, then fell back, weakened from the effort, and quickly fell back asleep.

Rebeca paused for a while to watch him, then took the cup, and headed out to do some neglected chores. Doreen and Gwen were just coming down the steps of Gwen's hut. Doreen had some empty dishes in her hands and Rebeca smiled.

"Now who is needing to feed people?"

Doreen chuckled, but changed the subject. "Have you got some clothing for Gwen?" Rebeca glanced at the dirt and blood stained clothes on the girl. Gwen looked down at herself and wrinkled her perfectly formed nose. Rebeca felt a twinge of jealousy and she shook herself as though she could easily rid herself of the unwelcome feeling. Rebeca swallowed hard and nodded her head.

"Her own clothes are washed and dried. I will get them, and the two of you can go to the river so Gwen can have a wash." Gwen opened her mouth to complain about the cold river, but shut it as she felt an overwhelming thankfulness at being back in safe surroundings.

Doreen and Gwen were soon at the river. Doreen only need a quick splash to refresh herself, and when she was finished, she turned around to give Gwen some privacy.

"Oooh! It's cold!" Gwen squealed. "We should have brought some hot water from the fire with us," she complained, her full lips pouting. A few minutes later, she was dressed in her own clothes and shoes, happily thinking about the deep, hot, bubbly bath she would soon be taking after her parents came to collect her. She turned to Doreen,

"When are my parents coming?"

"Are you finished, sweetheart?"

"Yes," Gwen said impatiently. "When are my parents coming?"

"I don't know, dear, I assume very soon." Doreen faced Gwen who gave a little 'huff' before stomping back to the village. Doreen raised an eyebrow as she looked at the clothes Gwen had abandoned on the ground. Bending down and scooping them up, she followed the girl, wondering how Gwen's parents would be contacted and if they would be able to help Doreen and her nephews get back to the airport.

CHAPTER 21

Loud voices greeted Doreen as she got back to the huts, and she was shocked to see four men in uniform pointing guns at the men, women and children, who were all gathered in a group by the fire. The men wore navy caps and blue shirts that said 'policia' on the left side. Gwen was off to the side with a fifth policeman, a terrified look on her face. As Doreen stepped forward, one of the policemen pointed a gun at her, and she dropped the clothes as she flung her hands up in the air.

Rebeca was speaking loudly in Spanish, making motions with her hands, pointing to Gwen. She had just seemed to calm down the situation, with the police lowering their guns, when Joe came around the back of one of the huts. Gwen and Doreen screamed as four guns focused on him and the man in front shouted.

"Alto!" Joe's face turned white as he stopped dead and threw up his hands. One of the men who seemed to be in charge, had a blue star on each of the epaulettes on his shoulders. He stepped forward and Joe stood in stunned silence as Rebeca called out, speaking quickly and motioning to him with her hands.

Finally, the inspector spoke in English, "Which one of you is Tadeo?" he said loudly.

"None of these are Tadeo," Rebeca spoke up in an exasperated voice. "He is gone."

The inspector turned to Gwen, who stood terrified. "Which one of these here is your kidnapper?"

"Nnnn … none …." her bottom lip quivered, "Rebeca is right, he left." He nodded to the others, and they all lowered their guns. As they did, Doreen and Joe slowly lowered their arms, but remained still.

"Where is my father?" asked Rebeca sharply, and Doreen suddenly realized they had not seen him for some time.

"He has been arrested for his part in this kidnapping," the man answered firmly.

"No!" called out Rebeca, "He did not do anything!"

"*We* will decide that," he answered.

"Are my parents coming?" A quiet voice spoke.

Everyone turned to Gwen, who was still looking frightened, but getting more and more anxious to leave the jungle and just go home; to her parents, her dog, her horse, and her bubble bath. There were a few moments of silence before the policeman spoke to her.

"They are flying to Managua right now. We are to bring you to la estacion de polica where they will be with you when you make your statement."

Rebeca pleaded with Gwen, "Tell them, Gwen, please! My father did not hurt you!"

"What's going on?" Toby stood at the entrance to his hut, holding onto the side as his shaky legs struggled to support him and he looked at everyone in a daze. Joe rushed over to him, and put his arm protectively around his brother to prevent him from falling over as he swayed on his weak, shaky legs.

"It's okay, Tobs," Joe comforted him. "It's time to go home, little brother."

The inspector spoke in Spanish to his team, and motioned around him to gather everyone who was involved in the incident. A few moments later, they were at the police pick-up trucks where they saw Rebeca's father sat in one, being guarded by another policeman. Gwen and Rebeca were put in that vehicle, and Doreen and Joe were in the other, with Toby in the middle, leaning heavily on Joe, drifting in and out of sleep. At each bump, Toby became more coherent and began asking questions.

"Shhhh, sweetheart," Doreen said, rubbing his shoulder. "Don't worry about anything at the moment. There is plenty of time for explanations. You are safe now, darling, you're safe. Just rest."

The pick-ups travelled quickly, and within a couple of hours, they were on the highway with Managua in the distance.

"Where are we?"

Doreen looked over as Toby spoke. His eyes looked sleepy but the colour had returned to his face, and as she touched his forehead with the back of her hand, she was pleased to find that his temperature was back to normal.

"We're in a police car," said Joe as he turned to look his brother in the eye. "Welcome back to the real world, bud!"

Toby lifted his head, and Joe helped him to a more comfortable sitting position as he and Doreen moved to make more space between them. Toby looked around, blinking slowly, and taking a deep breath.

"Why are we in a police car?" he asked groggily, frowning deeply. "How did I get here?" He paused, then looked around at Joe and Doreen, "How did *you* get here?"

Joe started to answer when Toby interrupted him. "I remember being in the jungle with a girl ... Gwen! Yes, it is coming back to me. Is she all right? Tadeo was after us. Where is Tadeo?" He blinked his eyes a couple of times. "Where is Emmie?"

Joe grinned widely, giving him a big hug. "Hang on, Tobs! Tell you what; we will tell the story from where Aunt Doreen, Rebeca and I found you. Then you can step back in time and tell us how you got there!" Doreen nodded in agreement, relieved to have her nephew nearly back to normal, and very relieved indeed, to be heading back to civilization.

"Perhaps you should start first, Aunt Dor," Joe looked at her, "You can start from where you picked up that weasel, Benito from the airport."

Doreen scowled at Joe and shook her head at his reprehensible attitude, pausing a moment before gathering her thoughts and beginning where she first encountered Toby's 'twin'. Joe's face clouded over as he heard how Benito had fooled his aunt and uncle, and it was all he could do to keep quiet while Doreen spoke.

Toby raised his eyebrows when Doreen got to the part about Rebeca preparing to give herself as a wife to save Gwen and him.

"Wow!" he said, overwhelmed by the courage of the unassuming girl who had nursed his wounds and taken care of Gwen and him.

"You got that right!" declared Joe, "She's some girl!"

Toby smiled at the faraway look that appeared in Joe's eyes. "I think my brother is in love," he laughed and Joe smiled. Immediately, Joe's countenance changed as he remembered Rebeca's look of disapproval at him, and he changed the subject.

"Carry on, Aunt Doreen," he encouraged.

By the time they pulled up in front of the police station, everyone knew the whole story, and they were talking animatedly over the last few days' adventure.

The policemen shepherded them all towards the door of the station, and Toby leaned into Joe for support as he walked slowly, mustering what strength he had. As they stepped inside, a well-dressed middle-aged couple brushed past them and Toby turned to see them gather Gwen into their arms in a tight huddle. He smiled to himself as he saw that Gwen's mother was indeed, as beautiful as she was.

"Oh darling! Thank goodness you're safe!"

The inspector gave them a few moments in their group hug, before nodding towards the door and saying, "Come inside, we need to get some details before we let you go. You'll have to stay in Managua for a couple of days, to make sure we have all the information we need."

After going over all the details of the events after Gwen's kidnapping, Toby remembered the diamonds in the Nintendo game. He looked in his backpack and discovered they were gone. Rebeca recounted finding his bag on the ground, and they came to the conclusion that Benito must have taken out the diamonds from the bag before abandoning it on the ground.

Rebeca's father had been released without charge, after Gwen and Toby convinced the authorities that although he had allowed Tadeo to bring the teenagers to his village, he had been bound by his obligation to Tadeo, and he and his daughter had been very kind to the captive teens. Toby was surprised at Gwen's altruism towards Rebeca and her father. Maybe the ordeal had been good for her!

The police also took into account the fact that Lucio had gone to Tudela to notify the police of the teenagers' whereabouts, and had waited there, to direct them to his village.

A few hours later, they were all sat in the penthouse suite of the Real Intercontinental Hotel, enjoying a bountiful meal and going over all the details again, to enlighten Lord Hugh and Lady Elizabeth Wentworth.

Toby hoped he would not have to say their names, as he was not sure if he was supposed to call them Mr and Mrs or Lord and Lady. He assumed calling them by their first names would be considered disrespectful. Lord Wentworth was a handsome, clean shaven man with emerald green eyes – the same as Gwen's, with light brown hair and just a little greying at the temples. Lady Elizabeth's blond hair was pulled back in a French braid that was tied with a deep blue ribbon that matched her sapphire eyes. He looked across the table at Gwen who had managed to slip into a deep bubble bath before the meal, and was now dressed in a simple plain green blouse that matched her eyes, and some cream cotton capris. Once again, he was struck at her beauty. She caught his gaze and as she smiled demurely, Toby's face grew warm and he turned away.

"Darling, first thing tomorrow, I am going to take you to the beauty spa downstairs. You must have that awful hair sorted out and get a facial and manicure. I've brought your make-up with me, so we can finish making you back into a beautiful young woman."

Gwen's smile immediately faded and she spoke softly, "Of course, Mummy."

Toby and Rebeca looked at each other and shook their heads. Poor Gwen. No wonder she was the way she was.

Lady Elizabeth turned to Rebeca, "We will sort out a car to take you and your father home. And of course, we will reimburse you financially for taking care of our daughter. How much would you like?"

The room went silent. Hugh sighed loudly and cleared his throat. "It is rather late for the two of you to head home now," he said to Lucio. "We have booked the floor beneath us, so you may each choose a room. You must all be tired. We can speak again in the morning when you all come up for breakfast."

Rebeca translated Hugh's words to her father, and he nodded reluctantly.

They all gladly stood, and after thanking the Wentworths for the meal, headed down the stairs to the next floor.

Toby was growing more exhausted by the minute and stumbled at the last step. Joe grabbed him, and held on to him until he got him in their room. He led Toby to a bed, and before he could ask him if he wanted to get undressed, Toby was sound asleep on the much welcome soft mattress and deep pillows.

CHAPTER 22

They awoke early the next morning, but no one was anxious to go back upstairs and be in the presence of chilly Lady Wentworth, so they spent an hour recounting the previous day's events, with a little bit of translating back and forth from Rebeca, and talking about everything except the couple upstairs.

Finally, Lucio stood up, taking charge. He spoke in Spanish, then nodded to Rebeca to translate.

"My father says it is time for us to go home. He is uncomfortable with these surroundings, so we will forgo the breakfast and just accept their gracious invitation for a car to take us home." She spoke softly, resting a glance on Toby who gave her a friendly grin. Again, a sadness filled her heart, and she hung her head slightly. Joe caught the sorrow in her eyes as she glanced at him, and a faint hope entered him. Maybe she did feel something for him after all – but what good was it if they were never to see each other again?

They walked as one, up the stairs and Doreen gave a firm knock on the door, her thoughts mulling over an idea that had begun forming the previous day. She had called Derrick to let him know they were safe and had put the idea to him. He said he trusted her and would agree with whatever she decided.

Lord Wentworth opened the door and smiled at them warmly. He spoke quietly, "I apologize for my wife's crassness yesterday. Sometimes she can be a little tactless, but she means well." He stepped back and stretched his right arm out to welcome them in. "Please, have a seat. Lady Wentworth and Gwen are just getting dressed."

They all walked in and as they sat on the leather couch and chairs, mother and daughter appeared in casual attire. Rebeca spoke first, addressing Lord Wentworth.

"My father thanks you for your offer of breakfast, and your very generous offer of a car to take us back to our village. However, he is anxious that we should return immediately to our home."

Hugh opened his mouth to speak, but before he could utter a word, Doreen turned to Rebeca who was sitting beside her and said firmly, "I have spoke to my husband and, if your father would permit it, we would like you to come and stay with us in Okotoks for a while … or as long as you would like. We could show you around and you could experience some of those things that you talked about."

A huge grin spread across Rebeca's face and she turned to her father, speaking excitedly in Spanish. There was only a brief pause before he narrowed his eyes, and nodded. She jumped up in delight and leaned over to give him a hug. He held her face in his hands and kissed her forehead, speaking in a gentle foreign tongue, but obviously speaking words of fatherly concern and love.

Suddenly, Rebeca's face clouded. "But I have no passport … or money … or … ," she looked down at her one dress that she wore, "clothes …"

Lady Wentworth smiled, "Now darling, those things are not a problem for us. You have taken good care of our daughter. We will sort out these 'little' problems easily. Give me a couple of days, and you will be ready to fly to Okotoks with your friends."

"Well, actually we fly to Calgary. Okotoks is a short drive from there," corrected Doreen.

Lady Wentworth waved her hand in the air dismissively as one used to getting her way. "Wherever it is, we can make sure you have what you need to get there."

Lucio was anxious to leave the western civilization and get back home to his tribe. He and Rebeca embraced tearfully and spoke a few more words in Spanish, then he and Lord Wentworth headed down to the lobby and out the door to the car that waited at the entrance. They shook hands firmly in silence, but with a deep understanding of fatherhood in each of their eyes, and parted company.

Lord Wentworth entered the suite as the others were sitting down to another generous supply of food. Suddenly, Toby remembered Emmie and smiled affectionately at the thought of her.

"What's that look for, Tobs?" Joe asked.

"I was just thinking about Emmie, my little capuchin friend. I will miss her. She took good care of me ..." he looked at Gwen and added, "... us. I suppose she is back with her family, eating mangoes for breakfast."

Rebeca took a slow deep breath before finally speaking, "I am sorry to tell you, Toby," she paused, not wanting to tell him what had happened to his little friend.

His smile vanished and he asked anxiously, "What? What is the matter?"

Rebeca swallowed hard before continuing. "I am afraid ... uh ... that your little friend was taken captive by Tadeo."

Toby looked confused. "Taken captive? But why? What good is a little monkey to him? I can't think that he would want a monkey for a pet."

Again, Rebeca sighed before answering, "Western people like little monkeys for pets." She paused a moment before adding, "It will not be for him. She will obtain a good price for him. Her friendship with you will increase her value because she will be easier to tame. She has already shown great intelligence and a caring attitude."

"No!" shouted Toby, and everyone's eyes were on him. He pounded the table angrily. "We have to go rescue her!"

Doreen looked at her nephew with understanding and affection. "Sweetheart, I understand that you want to help this little monkey, but you have to be realistic. We all need to go back home. Besides, we don't have the money to be traipsing around the world looking for her. I'm sorry, but that is just the way it is."

Again, Lady Wentworth interjected with a smile, "Of course you have money, Doreen. We are completely indebted to you and your family for rescuing our baby." She paused, stroking Gwen's hair. Gwen blushed in embarrassment of the term. "Whatever money you need, it is at your disposal." She smiled broadly, looking around the table at everyone.

Doreen look flustered, then turned back to Toby, "But you still have no idea where to begin looking; she could be anywhere!"

Just at that moment, Toby jumped as the mobile phone beeped in his pocket, startling him. He had forgotten he had charged it. His mind still on Emmie, he absently took out the phone and looked at it. He squinted his eyes in surprise.

"It's a message from Benito! He is in Florida with his uncle. He knows where Emmie is!"

⎯⎯➤●◄⎯⎯

THE END

Printed in Great Britain
by Amazon

THE TOBY MYERS ADVENTURES
BOOK 1

Finding Toby

Andy Hughes

After encountering Benito, a boy who looks strikingly similar to himself, Toby gets on a plane and somehow arrives not in Canada, his intended destination, but in Nicaragua. Here he is met by the boy's nefarious, gun-toting uncle who takes him captive. Escaping into the jungle, Toby soon ends up at the village where Benito's uncle is keeping Gwen, a rich young girl, hostage. Gwen and Toby attempt their escape together with the help of a native girl, Rebeca. Through the challenges and deadly adventures they face, the characters form a bond as they each journey through their own faith.

Other books by the same author:
Rescuing Emmie and *Saving Benito,*
available from Amazon

ISBN 979-8-391469-26-1

Cover design by Leah Hughes

RYAN MURPHY

YOU'VE GOT THE GIG!

100'000 miles as a cycle courier
in the Gig Economy

The Good, Bad & the Ugly